Was this what other people felt like when they had a family?

The door to the foyer opened and Jane appeared, her gaze landing on Colt with a look of surprise. She was beautiful standing there.

"Micha took off on me," Colt whispered. "I wasn't quick enough."

"She does do that," Jane whispered back, and she put one twin toddler down on the pew between them before reaching for the other. "Were you being a stinker, Michal Ann?"

Micha looked at her mother innocently as Jane scooped the toddler into her lap.

"I think you were," Jane whispered, but there was a smile tickling the corners of her lips. "Be nice to him, Micha. He's not used to this."

Jane looked over at him and smiled, and he felt that sense of camaraderie again. It felt good coming from her. It wasn't about pleasing a group or fitting in… It was just a moment between the two of them. Of all the people who had known him for years, Jane probably understood him best.

And that was dangerous ground…

Patricia Johns writes from Alberta, Canada. She has her Hon. BA in English literature and currently writes for Harlequin's Love Inspired and Heartwarming lines. You can find her at patriciajohnsromance.com.

Books by Patricia Johns

Love Inspired

Montana Twins

Her Cowboy's Twin Blessings
Her Twins' Cowboy Dad

Comfort Creek Lawmen

Deputy Daddy
The Lawman's Runaway Bride
The Deputy's Unexpected Family

His Unexpected Family
The Rancher's City Girl
A Firefighter's Promise
The Lawman's Surprise Family

Harlequin Heartwarming

A Baxter's Redemption
The Runaway Bride
A Boy's Christmas Wish
Her Lawman Protector

Visit the Author Profile page at Harlequin.com for more titles.

Her Twins' Cowboy Dad

Patricia Johns

HARLEQUIN® LOVE INSPIRED®

LOVE INSPIRED BOOKS

Recycling programs
for this product may
not exist in your area.

ISBN-13: 978-1-335-47916-7

Her Twins' Cowboy Dad

Copyright © 2019 by Patricia Johns

www.Harlequin.com

Printed in U.S.A.

The king's heart is in the hand of the Lord,
as the rivers of water:
he turneth it whithersoever he will.
—*Proverbs* 21:1

To my husband, whom I love more every day.
The years together only make it sweeter.

Chapter One

Colt Hardin stood by a window on the second floor of an office building in downtown Creekside, Montana, cowboy hat under one arm, trying to calm his thoughts as he looked out over the street. The building itself was only three stories, but it was the highest one in that little ranching town. A few pickup trucks slowed to a stop at the streetlight, windows rolled down to let in the warm July breeze. One of the trucks had an old dog in the back, trotting back and forth along the truck bed. The light changed to green, and the trucks rolled forward again. Colt preferred trails and fields, horseback or the rattling old ranch truck. Town was just too busy for his liking.

Colt tapped his hat against his thigh, attempting to quiet that jitter inside him. Uncle Beau passed away a few days ago, and he had been called to the lawyer's office for the reading of the will. If Uncle Beau hadn't changed anything, Colt was inheriting it all.

Old Beau had been a complicated guy in life—a good rancher and a neighbor who could be counted on when weather went bad or times got tough. He was gruff, stubborn, often narrow-minded, but with a sensitive side that had surprised Colt more than once. But as kind as he could be to a neighbor, he was unmovable when it came to family. Once his mind was made up about someone, there was no changing it, and that character flaw had torn apart the family. It was only because those relationships were in tatters that Colt was set to inherit everything.

Beau's marriage to his aunt had shown him that marriage was difficult…and, it turned out, so was keeping any kind of functional relationship with a man's kids. Josh was an only child—it shouldn't have been that complicated. And Colt didn't have his own father in his life, so Beau had been the closest he'd had to a dad. That wasn't a sweet sentiment, either, because Beau was the main reason he'd been steering clear of getting married and starting a family of his own.

A patter of little shoes came up the stairs, and Colt glanced over as two redheaded toddlers in matching floral-print dresses emerged into the hallway and immediately scampered in opposite directions. A slim woman with dark hair pulled into a messy bun at the back of her head appeared behind them and jogged after the squealing toddler who dashed down the hall, while the other little girl headed in his direction. The woman wore a pink sundress that fluttered behind her in a wave, and he couldn't help but wonder how she'd catch both children.

The little girls had flaming-red curls that bounced at the sides of their heads in matching pigtails… Some distant relative of Beau Marshall, perhaps? The Marshalls were known for their fiery red hair. Colt was related to Beau through Beau's wife's side of the family, so his hair was a dark brown that women made a point of telling him shone auburn in the sunlight.

The woman scooped up the giggling girl and came back down the hall, a bag bouncing against one hip and the toddler secured on the other.

"Michal, come back here…" the woman called to the toddler who'd dashed in his direction, and the tiny girl looked up at Colt for a moment, round brown gaze meeting his soberly. She took a step to the side to head around him and he matched her, eyeing her with a small smile. He could see the mischief in that little face.

"Could you just head her off?" the woman asked, hoisting the other toddler a little higher in her arms as she approached. "She's quick."

"I'll try," he said. The toddler swerved past him and he shot an arm out, scooping the youngster up as she let out a surprised squeak. She was as light as a barn cat, and those little legs gave a couple of kicks as he spun her around to face her mother, then handed her over.

"Thanks." The woman's face broke into a smile as she gathered the second toddler in her arms. "I thought it was hard to carry around two car seats. I had no idea how bad it would be once they were walking."

"I can only imagine," he said with a short laugh. "Michael—that's an odd name for a girl."

"I liked it." She gave him a tired smile. "It's Biblical. David's first wife."

"Oh, right." Yeah, he vaguely remembered that. Not Michael, but Michal.

She looked over at the lawyer's office door, then down at a scrap of paper in one hand that she could just see past the toddler. Colt noticed the building address written in cursive, followed by the office number.

"Are you here to see Mr. Davis?" Colt asked.

She nodded. "You, too?"

"Yeah. I'm Colt Hardin. And you are…?"

The color drained from her face and she licked her lips. Did she recognize his name? "Jane Marshall. Pleasure."

"So you're…a relative of Beau's?" he asked, and his stomach sank. There weren't too many Marshalls left—at least not in name. It seemed like every Marshall family had girl after girl, and after they married and took their husbands' names there was yet another branch of the family tree without the Marshall name. Beau had complained about it to no end.

"My husband was Josh Marshall," she replied. "He died, but Beau Marshall was his father."

Josh—his cousin. Colt's heart stuttered, then hammered to catch up. So this was the wife—but he didn't even know that Josh had had kids. None of the family had ever seen pictures of his wife—Josh had only announced his marriage and then gone silent. This woman was slim, with dark hair and pale skin. She was pretty, but rumpled. Her pink sundress tugged up at one hip where she held Michal, and the other toddler was pulling at a loose thread at her shoulder.

"You're Josh's wife?" Colt repeated. His voice sounded choked in his own ears.

She nodded. "I am. And you're his cousin. Josh told me about you."

That was almost more than he could say. When Josh took off for the city, he'd cut contact with all of them except for an email once every few years with some pertinent information, like when he joined the army and when he got married. And the army had told them when Josh was killed… So Colt had heard absolutely nothing about her besides the fact that she'd married into the family.

"What was your name, again?" he asked.

"Jane Marshall," she replied. "This is Susanna and Michal, or Suzie and Micha for short."

"They have the Marshall look," he said. The fiery red hair that hung in curls around those identical, chubby faces, for one. "But Josh died, what, three years ago?"

"They *are* Marshalls," she replied, her tone hardening just a touch. "Josh never got to meet them. He…" She swallowed. "He died before they were born."

"He never told us—" he said.

"Yes, he did. He told his father I was pregnant," she cut him off. "Beau contacted me once after they were born."

"Really." Beau had never mentioned it to him, and they'd worked together daily for twenty years. Beau had complained often enough about his ungrateful son.

So there had been granddaughters that Beau had never made reference to. That was just like the man—keep Colt working like a horse and never tell him anything that might interfere with his dedication to the ranch. Because Josh wasn't any help at all having left for the city, and Colt had been the one to shoulder the responsibility of keeping this ranch running all these years. Beau's health had only been getting worse, and he'd been handing off more and more of the daily running of the place until Colt was doing just about everything. Beau had promised Colt ten years ago that he'd leave him the ranch, keep it in the family. In fact, that was what pushed Josh away to begin with, when Beau told him that if he wasn't going to take ranching seriously, he'd cut him out of the will. Not a single acre would go to Josh, Beau had vowed, but now that Josh's widow was here for the reading of the will, he had to wonder if Beau had been stringing him along all these years.

Anything was possible with Beau.

The office door opened and Steve Davis, a portly older gentlemen, poked his head out. Colt knew the lawyer relatively well. There weren't too many lawyers in Creekside, and he attended the same church that Colt did. Steve had been at the funeral.

"Colt, again, I'm so sorry for your loss," he said, holding out his hand.

"Thank you." Colt stepped forward and shook Steve's hand. "I appreciate it."

"And you must be Jane?" Steve asked turning to the woman beside him.

"Yes, that's me." She hitched a toddler higher on her hip. "I hope bringing the girls with me wasn't a problem."

"No, of course not," Steve said. "Let's go into my office."

Colt stood back as Jane passed into the office first. Micha stared at him with those big brown eyes as she passed, while Suzie seemed more interested in trying to squirm out of her mother's arms. He stepped into the office after Jane, then pulled the door shut behind him. Jane took a seat in front of Steve's wide desk and dug in her shoulder bag, emerging with a ziplock bag of crackers.

Colt eased into the seat next to her, and he watched as she doled out crackers into the toddlers' hands. They sat down on the floor, two crackers each, and set to munching on them.

"You were the only people mentioned in Beau Marshall's will," Steve began. "Colt, you were named, as well as his grandchildren. After Josh's death, Beau updated his will so that their mother would be conservator of their inheritance if he were to die while they were still minors."

"He knew about them," Colt said woodenly.

"Yes," Steve confirmed. "He did. He spoke to me about them after they were born."

"Josh told him about my pregnancy," Jane said. "Josh died when I was about six months pregnant and he was deployed. Anyway, I emailed Beau with a couple of pictures once they were born. I think Josh would have wanted that."

"Did anyone else know?" Colt asked, still trying to make sense of all of this in his head. How much had his uncle been hiding from him?

"Not that I know of," Steve replied. "Beau was a man who kept his own counsel. I think you know that." Steve opened a file folder and looked between Colt and Jane.

"A conservator—what does that mean?" Jane asked.

"It means that you will be able to manage your daughters' inheritance as you see fit and split the remainder of it between them when they turn eighteen."

"Oh…"

"Let's get started, shall we?" Steve said.

Colt looked over at Jane, and she glanced toward him at the same time. She looked nervous—her lips were pale and she was fidgeting with that plastic bag of crackers. He knew what Beau had promised him, but he also knew exactly how far Beau could be trusted. Somehow, after Josh left because of this will and all the pain the family went through surrounding it, Colt hadn't considered the idea that Beau might change the will completely. But it was possible.

"To Colt Hardin, my nephew, I leave the ranch," Steve read, his voice calm and quiet, and Colt felt a wave of relief. "I leave him all of the land, the buildings and the debt that has accrued over the years. Of anyone, Colt will be able to make something of it. I'm pleased to keep this ranch in the family."

The ranch. *Thank You, God.* He knew the land was mortgaged to the hilt, but if everything just continued as it was, he could work his way out of debt. The ranch was his. Uncle Beau had done as he'd promised, and Colt could go on running this ranch like he'd hoped.

Steve turned toward Jane. "And to my grandchildren, the children of my only son, Joshua Marshall, I leave the herd to be split between them equally."

The lawyer's words hung in the air, and Colt felt like his breath had been knocked out of his chest. Beau had left Colt the land, but he'd given his toddler granddaughters the *cattle*? How on earth was he supposed to run a floundering ranch when he didn't own the actual animals? Beau had kept his promise, all right. Colt had the land. But without that herd, without the income at market time, Colt could lose it all.

Jane stared at the lawyer as the moment seemed to slow down and stretch out in front of her. She'd had no idea what Josh's dad had left to her girls, but the fact that he'd named them in his will had felt like an answer to prayer when she'd gotten the call. Jane didn't know what she'd been hoping for, besides some family connection for her daughters. She had some death benefits from the military, but most of that had been soaked up in paying off debt. Josh had been a spender—when he got home, he didn't want to worry about "bills and stuff." He just wanted to enjoy the American Dream. So now she was proudly debt free, but very little was left over besides the monthly payments that came to her. And twins were expensive to raise. She had to find a way to provide for her daughters because her job with a maid service had just ended. But cattle?

"What does that mean, exactly?" Jane asked hesitantly. "He gave my daughters cows?"

The lawyer nodded. "Yes."

"How many cows are in the herd, exactly?" she asked.

The lawyer smiled indulgently. "Currently, it consists of four hundred and eighty cows."

"What am I supposed to do with them?" she asked feebly.

Micha put a sodden cracker into Jane's hand, and she instinctively closed her fingers around it.

"That's where you have some decisions to make," Mr. Davis replied. "You have a few options. Once the paperwork is finalized, of course."

"Of course…" she breathed. "But what options?"

"You could sell the herd back to Colt here, for one," Mr. Davis replied. "Or you could move the herd to another ranch, if you own one."

"I don't," she murmured.

"Or you could work out some other deal with Colt."

Jane looked over at Colt, but his expression was granite. He was staring at a spot on the carpet between his boots. Right now, she didn't even know where she was going to stay. She was homeless with two little girls and nothing but the hope of an inheritance to sustain her. She could feel the tears rising up inside her.

"First things first, though," Mr. Davis said cheerily.

"It's going to take a week before all of this becomes finalized. Then you can both talk to your banks and decide upon a course of action."

"The inheritance is for my girls, though," Jane said. "You said I'm allowed to sell the cattle?"

"Beau has his will set up in such a way that you, as their mother, can manage their inheritance—the cattle or the money gotten from the sale of them—until they are eighteen. At which point, whatever is left will be divided between them. He wanted to make sure that you could provide for them in their formative years."

"Okay…" That was particularly kind of her late father-in-law. Jane didn't want to deprive her girls of their rightful inheritance from their grandfather, but she did need to care for the girls in the meantime. At least there was some ability for her to do that.

"Why did he do this?" Colt broke in.

"That's a good question," Jane agreed. "We're going to have cattle and nowhere to put them, and Colt is going to have a ranch and no cattle!"

"I think that's the point, isn't it?" Mr. Davis asked. "An earlier version of the will had the cattle going to Josh, not the girls. Beau was hoping that when he passed on, Josh might…come home."

"And we'd work together," Colt concluded.

"Yes," Mr. Davis said with a nod. "That was his hope."

Colt grunted, and Jane glanced over at him again. If this had been a plan to reunite the cousins, it was too late for that.

"So why leave the cattle to my daughters after my husband died?" Jane asked.

"The ranch was remortgaged," Mr. Davis said. "There was a lot of debt, and he didn't want to cut his grandchildren out of his will. He didn't have any cash to leave to them, and quite honestly, he was hoping that after a few years, he'd have built up a little more wealth, gotten past the rough patch. Then he could have reworked his will again. He didn't get the chance, unfortunately. This was his worst-case scenario, I'm afraid, but he still hoped that his granddaughters would have a connection with the family again."

"He wanted my girls to know their family," she breathed.

"That's what he told me." Mr. Davis smiled gently. "But that's no pressure on you, okay? We all have a certain number of years in our lifetimes in order to make up for our mistakes. Beau ran out of time, as sad as that is. But that doesn't mean that you owe him anything."

No, she didn't owe Beau anything—he'd done nothing more than send her a couple of emails after the girls were born, neither of which had been terribly warm. She could see where her husband's emotional distance had come from. She'd loved Josh dearly, but being his wife hadn't been easy. If nothing else, by her brief communication with Beau, she'd understood why her husband had been so unwilling to reconnect with his father. But still, her daughters had family out here—and that would mean something to them one day. Their cantankerous grandfather was dead, but there were other family members that the girls might want to know. Perhaps even their "uncle" Colt. He was a relative, at least, and being considerably older than them, she wasn't sure what else to call him.

Suzie clutched at Jane's dress and she absently reached down to pick the toddler up. She'd come to the town of Creekside on faith. Josh's death had been difficult to deal with. Those vows had tied them together on a deep level, and while being married to Josh had been hard, she couldn't just walk away from him when it got tough, either. He'd never been an easily affectionate man, but she'd known how much he loved her. The stuff he saw in the army had left wounds that never healed, and she had only wanted to support him, let him know that she'd love him no matter what. Jane hadn't realized how much of herself she'd lost as she struggled to maintain her marriage until she was forced to look at life without her husband in it. Coming out to Creekside was both an act of faith and a desperate leap. She'd take anything God provided. She'd come all the way from Minneapolis with her toddlers in the back of a ten-year-old sedan to see what God had in store.

And right now, she had to wonder if that had been a mistake. Maybe she should have stayed in Minneapolis and put her energy into finding an apartment instead of driving out here on a wish and a prayer. But what did she have to stay for? The house was gone. She'd been laid off from her job. She could have afforded to rent a tiny apartment while she tried to sort out her future... But that phone call from the polite Montana lawyer had sparked some hope inside her. He wouldn't say what the girls had been left, but he'd said it was part of the ranch, and he called it *significant, and definitely worth coming out*. Her husband had told her that his dad had cut him out of the will, so this was completely unexpected, and she'd had nothing at all to lose.

"I realize that you both have a lot of thinking to do, plans to make," Mr. Davis said, standing up. "For my part, I'll get these papers submitted and that will put the land into your name, Colt, and the cattle into yours,

Jane. Unless you have any other questions, I believe that takes care of our business today."

They were being dismissed. Jane smoothed a hand over Suzie's soft curls, and her heart sank inside her. She had enough money for a few nights in a cheap hotel, and then she was out of cash. She had an emergency credit card, but she was afraid to start using it. She knew firsthand just how easy it was to slide back into debt. What she needed was a job that would allow her to care for her daughters at the same time. That was a tall order…especially out here in Creekside, Montana, where she knew absolutely no one.

"Thank you," Jane said, reaching out to shake hands with the lawyer.

"Thanks, Steve." Colt did the same.

Jane picked up her bag and rooted out sippy cups of juice for the girls. Sometimes keeping their hands full helped them to cooperate a little better. Jane guided the girls toward the door. Colt got there before her, and he opened it and let her pass through first.

In the hallway, the girls clambered toward the window that overlooked the street. They weren't tall enough to look out, but someone had left a magazine there, and they squatted down next to it, playing with the glossy pages. Even though Jane couldn't see it from where she stood, she knew that her car was parked just outside that window, packed to the gills with everything she owned.

"Did you know what was coming?" Colt asked as he pulled the door shut behind them. He was a handsome man, but not in the same way her husband had been. Josh had been full of laughter and jokes, while Colt looked more serious. Josh's hair had been the same bright red as his daughters'.

"No, I had no idea," she replied, tearing her gaze away from him. "Although, I think you expected to get the ranch."

Colt didn't say anything, but those dark eyes drilled into hers. She sighed. What was she going to do—pick up her late husband's fight with his family? Beau could leave that land to anyone he chose, and he hadn't chosen Josh.

"Your uncle was an interesting man, wasn't he?" she said after a moment.

"You don't know the half of it," Colt growled.

"Losing the cattle isn't good for you, is it?" she asked.

"No," he admitted. "I know your husband was cut from the will, but I worked my tail off on that land. I don't have much else, either. So cutting the herd out from under me isn't good for me at all."

"I'm sorry about that." And she was. "I suppose you could sell, too, if you needed to."

"Not a chance," he retorted. "I've worked that land with Beau for twenty years. I've invested too much into the ranch, and I'm finding a way to hold on to it. Beau wanted that land in family hands."

"Yes, Josh told me about that." She could sense some bitterness there when Colt mentioned Josh. She'd known there had been a lot of family tension, but she hadn't been sure what she'd walk into, exactly.

"It was Beau's choice, not mine," Colt said.

"I know…" She sighed. "What do we do? I'm serious. I have no idea how to even start. I mean—"

"We wait," he interrupted. "We have to get everything in our names first."

"Yes, but then what?" she pressed. "I assume you'll want your cattle back."

"Yeah, that would be good," he said, and a wry smile turned up one corner of his lips. "I'll have to talk to the bank and see if I can get a loan…and buy you out."

"How much are four hundred and eighty head of cattle worth?" she asked.

"A fair bit."

"Oh…" Jane's gaze moved over to where her daughters were playing, their sippy cups on the floor next to them. It was a relief to know that her daughters would be provided for. She felt guilty enough using the death benefits to pay off all the debt. There was nothing left to put aside for them. Josh would have wanted them to have something.

"Where are you staying?" Colt asked.

"I don't know yet," she replied, and she felt her chin tremble and tears well in her eyes. She looked away, trying to hide the rise of emotion.

"Are you okay?" Colt asked, his tone dropping.

"I'm—" She swallowed hard. "I'll figure it out."

"I saw a car out the window—packed full of everything but the kitchen sink," he said. "That yours?"

Jane managed to blink back the tears and she nodded. "That's mine."

"Are you moving out to Montana? Is this just a short trip? I'm just wondering how things stand."

"I'm not sure yet," she said honestly. "It's been really hard since Josh died. We'd just bought a house that needed a lot of work, and I couldn't make the payments alone. Josh's death benefits helped me to get out of debt, but I had to sell the house. So… I haven't decided where is best to land right now. I know that the way your uncle split this isn't good for you, but him remembering my girls—it's going to help a lot."

"Hmm." Colt nodded slowly. "Look, I'm not thrilled that my uncle did it this way, but this doesn't have to be the end of the world for me. We'll just have to iron it out. Are you willing to let me buy the herd back from you?"

"Yes, definitely. I have no use for cattle."

"I'd really like to get this taken care of as quickly as possible. I have some cows ready for market, and keeping this ranch afloat relies on that income. So the sooner I can get this sorted out with you, the better. Can you afford to stay in town for a couple of weeks?"

Jane sighed and looked away. "Not comfortably."

"Do you need to get back?" he asked, narrowing his eyes. "Because I have an idea. I don't want to overstep, but if you want a place to stay until it's resolved, you are welcome to stay at the ranch."

"Are you sure you want us underfoot?" she asked. "We're strangers."

"I want to buy back my cattle," he replied. "And if having you underfoot makes that happen faster, I'm happy with it." He shot her a wry smile. "I don't bite. Technically, I'm family."

Family—Josh's family, at least. She'd never met these people in her three years of marriage to Josh, or in the three years since his death. They were just a jumble of stories she'd heard. Beau might have wanted some sort of family reconciliation, but that didn't mean the rest of the Marshalls did.

"I don't want to stay for free," she countered.

"If you really wanted to pitch in, we need to clean out Beau's house. If you'd help me with that, I'd be grateful. Beau's sister is staying with me for a few weeks while we clean it out, but she has a few health issues, and I'm not sure how much she can get done on her own…"

"That might be a bit personal. I didn't know Beau," she said. "Are you comfortable with me going through his things? Would his sister be okay with that?"

"She'll be fine with it. She wasn't really eager to do the job, either. She and Beau had a falling out some years ago. She's willing to help me, personally, but…" He sighed. "Look, maybe you'll find some stuff that pertains to Josh. As for me, I don't have time to do it all myself, and as Peg can tell you, Beau wasn't real close to that many people. Everyone who wanted a keepsake from Beau has already taken something. The rest just needs to be boxed up for Goodwill."

"Well…" She paused for a moment to consider. Maybe there would be some hints about Josh's childhood, or pictures that might be nice to keep for the girls. Who knew? This was her chance to connect with her late husband's family, for better or for worse. And with Peg on the scene, she wouldn't be alone on a ranch with this uncomfortably handsome Colt.

"Where would I stay?" she asked.

"There's an in-law suite in the basement of the house," he said. "It's got a whole separate entrance and everything, and that's where I live. So you and the girls can stay with Peg upstairs in Beau's place. What do you say?" he asked, fixing her with his dark gaze.

What choice did she have?

"I'd be happy to."

Chapter Two

Colt led the way back to the Marshall ranch, Jane driving in her little silver sedan behind his red Chevy. Maybe it would be known as the Hardin ranch from now on, and he could take down the sign and put up a new one. He wasn't ready for that yet, though. This still felt like Beau's land, and he still felt like the nephew who should be grateful. And he was—he always had been. Maybe a little guilty, too, because he'd known all along that his uncle was making a mistake in his fight with his son. Both Beau and Josh had been stubborn idiots. And now Jane was in the middle of it all, and he felt a little sorry for her. This family's problems had nothing to do with her, and he really hoped that he hadn't reacted too badly... Had he? He couldn't help but wonder how she was feeling about all of this.

The pasture on either side of the highway rolled out in low, green hills. Cattle grazed, tails flicking, and Colt's practiced gaze estimated that the calves were already triple in size from when they were born. As he drove, he kept an eye on the strip of barbed wire fencing, looking for holes or weak areas. He'd always done this, but today, it felt like an honor instead of just the smart thing to do. This was *his* land now. He was still wrapping his mind around that.

Colt glanced back at her car in the rearview mirror. Jane was still there, pacing him as they sped down the cracked highway. He'd wanted this—not his uncle's death, but definitely a chance at running his own ranch. Beau had promised to leave him the ranch for years— reiterating it every time he ranted about his son's life choices—but Colt had always imagined butting heads with the old guy for a good many years longer than this. Beau's fatal stroke had taken everyone by surprise. Colt might have worked this land, but Beau had built it up from a few scrubby acres into the viable ranch it was today. Viable, and underwater with a second mortgage. His uncle had been open with him about the financial situation, at least, if not about his plans for his will. Hopefully Beau hadn't been hiding anything else.

Strange to think that Beau had put so much thought into reconciling him and Josh, though. Why not reconnect with his son himself? But Colt could appreciate that Josh's daughters would benefit by the will. It might complicate Colt's life right now, but it had been the right thing to do.

The Marshall ranch was about half an hour's drive outside Creekside. He had driven a little slower than usual to make sure that Jane could keep up with him, and as the turn came up for the ranch, he slowed and signaled.

The drive wound around a copse of trees and led to the single-story ranch house. It was painted white, with a traditional wraparound veranda. There was a strip of basement windows showing—and those were the windows that let some light into Colt's part of the house. He parked in his regular spot beside Beau's black truck, and Jane pulled up next to him. As he hopped out of the truck, Jane's car door opened, too, and she got out of the car and looked around herself.

"Wow," she breathed. "This is gorgeous."

He followed her gaze. The front yard had a couple of ancient birch trees towering overhead, providing sun-dappled shade in the July sunlight, and beyond were the fields that stretched out in undulating hills, warmed by the summer sunshine. A sheet of sparrows flapped up from a copse of trees in the distance, billowed, then landed again.

"It's a beautiful area," he agreed.

Jane opened the back door of her car and disappeared inside as she unbuckled the toddlers. Some local ladies had dropped off some casseroles for him, so he had food to feed her, at least. He wasn't sure how much tuna casserole a toddler would consume, but he'd leave the problem up to Jane. She was best equipped to handle it anyway.

The side door to the house opened and Aunt Peg, as she preferred to be called, poked her curly iron-gray head out.

"You're back. And you brought company, I see," Peg said. She always sounded no-nonsense, and it was hard to tell if she was approving or not, much like her brother had been.

"Yep, this is Josh's wife, Jane," Colt said. "And his little girls."

Peg blinked at him, straightened and then stepped outside, letting the screen door bang shut behind her.

"Josh's family?" Peg said, her voice tight. "Really?"

Peg wore a flour-powdered apron over a '70s-style housedress, and she came closer, peering into the car until Jane emerged with one of the toddlers. She put the girl down and shot Peg a smile.

"Hi, I'm Jane."

"Pleasure." Peg have her a nod.

"She's here for a week or so while we iron out an inheritance issue," Colt said. "She'll stay upstairs with you, if you don't mind."

"We'll work something out." Peg pressed her lips together into a thin line. "What's the issue with the will?"

"Beau left me the land, and he left the cattle to Jane's daughters," Colt said. "So Jane is going to stay with us while we get that ironed out. I need to buy the cattle back."

A smile of amusement tickled the corners of Peg's lips. "You'd almost think he was trying to get you married off, wouldn't you?"

To his cousin's widow? Not likely. Josh's estrangement from the family had been an endless source of upset around here, and Colt highly doubted that his uncle would have wanted that. It might not have been logical because Josh got married a few years after he left home, but Beau blamed "the wife" as much as anyone else for his son's refusal to talk to him. Anything but admit it was his own fault.

"It had a whole lot less to do with me, and more to do with wanting to fix things with Josh," Colt replied. Besides, Colt wasn't interested in marriage, and Beau had known why.

Jane emerged from the car with the second toddler, and she slammed the door shut.

"Well…these would be my great-nieces, then," Peg

said, softening immediately. "Do they ever look like their father."

They did, and if Josh hadn't been killed, he would have loved being a dad. He'd always had that gentle-giant quality about him, and with his jovial sense of humor, Colt could see him sliding easily into being a family man.

Aunt Peg scooped up one of the toddlers in her arms, looking the girl over from head to toes.

"That's Micha," Jane said. "This here is Suzie."

"We might as well go inside," Peg said. "I cleaned up the kitchen, Colt. You're welcome."

Colt had started to expand a little bit in the house—and he'd made his breakfast upstairs in Beau's place. He'd left some oatmeal out for Peg. Maybe it would be best to keep to his own space until Peg went back home.

"Sorry about that," he said with a short laugh. He hadn't left it in a mess or anything.

Colt followed the women into the house, letting the screen door bang shut behind him. The house felt different with Beau gone. The kitchen was as it always had been—just the way Beau's late wife, Sandra, had kept it. She'd been a good cook, unlike Peg, who never did get the touch.

"Aunt Peg, I asked Jane if she'd give you a hand with emptying out the house," Colt said.

"Did you think of asking me what I thought of that?" Peg retorted. She put down the toddler, who beelined back to Jane.

"It's my house now, Peg," he said, but he sent his aunt a tired smile to show her he wasn't taking it to heart. "I figured it might help. If you'd rather do it alone, I mean—"

"No, no," Peg said, sadness filling her eyes. She pulled a dish of what appeared to be apple crisp off the counter and deposited it onto the table along with a serving spoon. "I don't want to do it alone. Besides…" She looked down at the toddlers. "There's family to get acquainted with, isn't there?"

"I didn't know Beau," Jane said quietly. "But he did remember my girls in his will, and I'm grateful for that."

"Did Josh talk about us?" Peg asked.

"A little," Jane replied.

"Did he mention why he left and never wanted to come back?" Peg asked, and Colt felt his chest constrict. Did they have to do this—with a relative stranger? He, for one, didn't want to talk about it.

Color rose in Jane's cheeks, but she didn't answer.

"Ah, so he did," Peg went on, then sighed. "Beau wasn't as bad as he seemed, my dear. We're all just human."

Colt couldn't help but feel like he'd been the one to chase off his cousin. Josh and Beau had been at odds for years. Josh wanted to join the army and his father had wanted him to stay home and work the land. For most families that wouldn't be relationship ending, but for the stubborn Marshalls it snowballed into a bigger and bigger issue, picking up the detritus of every single disagreement they'd ever had. Josh wasn't the kind of son Beau wanted. Beau wanted a son to take over the ranch. Well, Colt wanted a chance at that life, and Beau was more than happy to teach him the ropes.

Was it wrong of Colt to take advantage of that? Probably. While Josh's father was alive, someone had to run this place, and Josh hadn't been interested. But Beau told his son that when he died, the land wouldn't be sold so that Josh could use the money for his own goals—Josh wouldn't inherit at all. When it came right down to it, Beau could leave the ranch to anyone he chose, but the cost of that had been a splintered family. Standing here in his newly inherited kitchen, it didn't feel quite so satisfying as Colt had imagined it would. This was all his, and he couldn't help but feel like a cheat.

He was glad Jane was here, and that her daughters would get something. It would even the score a little bit. Make it right.

"It really isn't my business," Jane said and she dropped her gaze. Josh had gone on and on about that inheritance, and she'd simply put it out of her mind. There was money tied up in land that would never come to them. Wasn't a life together worth more than cash? But it had hurt her husband deeply because it meant that his father didn't respect his goals in life and didn't love him enough to leave him anything. For Josh it was about the money and his father's respect, and for his dad it was about the land. Period. Josh never made his peace with it.

Jane bent down to dig out that zippered bag of crackers again, mostly as an excuse not to look at them. There was so much sadness and frustration in this home that she could actually feel it in the air, and she shivered.

"We missed Josh," Peg said, her voice trembling a little. "There was a hole here—it never filled in. My brother might have had his faults, but he did love his son something fierce. If Josh looked to punish him for his sins, he sure succeeded."

And maybe Josh *had* been trying to punish his family. He hadn't wanted Jane anywhere near them. That hadn't been her choice, though. She'd wanted family, and she'd wanted to know his, too, even if there was tension and bickering. People didn't hatch from eggs, and she'd felt certain that she would have understood her husband better if she could have met the family that raised him. Maybe their marriage could have been a little bit easier, if she did. Here was her chance, apparently. A little late, but still a chance to understand the man she'd married.

Colt cleared his throat, and an awkward silence filled the kitchen. Jane gave the girls each another cracker to munch on, and she wondered if she'd made a mistake in coming here. This family had baggage and they'd be sorting through it now that Beau had passed away. She didn't belong in the middle of this mess. Josh was gone, after all.

There was always that reserve credit card if she decided to stay in a cheap hotel.

Peg sighed. "I'm going to go set up one of the guest bedrooms. Can the girls sleep with you in a double bed?"

"This seems like a sensitive time for the family," Jane said. "I can easily stay in town. Colt was kind enough to offer, but I can see that—"

"You think *this* is tense?" Peg asked with an abrupt laugh.

"A little…" Jane murmured.

"Jane, you're the only connection we've got to Josh now. And maybe you'll be able to give us some insights, too. You're family. You're very welcome here. I come across a bit harshly, or so I've been told. Is that it?"

"No, not at all…" Jane said. Now was not the time to admit to that.

"Now, about the sleeping arrangement for the little ones," Peg said.

"Yes, I could have them sleep with me," she conceded. "Thank you. I appreciate it."

"Not at all."

That prim, downturned mouth never changed expression as Peg headed out of the kitchen, leaving Jane and Colt alone with the little girls.

"I really did try to get Beau to call his son," Colt said. "It was never my intention to get between them."

"But you managed to," she replied, raising her gaze. "I don't want to get in the middle of this, and I have no interest in this ranch...but Josh felt completely abandoned by both of you. You ganged up on him."

"Not the case," Colt said, and his voice softened a little. "Josh hated ranching. He thought it was boring. He wanted excitement, and that wasn't here with the cattle. He didn't want this life, and ranching was in Beau's blood."

"And yours, it would seem," she said.

"I'm not going to apologize for that," he replied with a shake of his head. "I'm a cowboy to the bone. I love the early mornings, the physical work, the cattle, the smell, the rhythms of the seasons. This is the life I've always wanted, and I'm not going to pretend it means less to me than it does."

"Josh didn't like that stuff," she admitted. "I know that. I'm sorry. I'm not trying to pick a fight with you."

"For Beau it was about the ranching legacy," Colt said.

"Josh was his son," Jane said quietly. "*He* wanted to be his father's legacy. Not some land."

Colt met her gaze for a moment, then nodded. "I

know. You're right. Like I said, I never meant to get between them. Beau and I might have had the ranching in common, but we butted heads about everything else. He was a stubborn man."

"Peg joked about Beau trying to get you married, though," Jane said. "It sounds like you two were pretty close, in spite of it all."

"Getting me married," Colt said with a short laugh. "That would be ironic. I'm not the marrying kind, and Beau knew that. From what I can see, marriage is a piece of paper—nothing more."

Jane looked at him, curious, but afraid to ask. Where Colt stood on the idea of marriage really wasn't her business.

"Look, this family has its own set of problems," Colt went on. "My aunt died in a swimming accident when Josh and I were teenagers, but Sandra and Beau were never happy. They fought constantly, and my family hated Beau for obvious reasons."

"Obvious?" she said.

"He was a jerk to her, and everyone knew it. But Sandra gave as good as she got. Those two could barely stand each other." He sighed. "I can't point out too many happy couples in this family."

Colt was bitter—that much was obvious. But she didn't agree with him. "Marriage *is* more than a piece of paper. I've been married. I know what those vows mean."

"No offense, but I don't see it."

"Commitment matters," Jane countered with a shake of her head. "There is a difference between staying together for a lifetime because you chose it at the beginning, and staying together because you just didn't break up yet. To be able to promise to stand by each other, no matter what—"

"People can promise that without the ceremony. Do you think a piece of paper makes those promises any stronger?" he retorted.

"Maybe not the paper, but the vow before God should," she said. "In my experience there's a vast difference between a boyfriend and a husband."

Jane had stood by her husband. If it weren't for those vows, she might not have had the strength. Vows mattered.

Colt eyed her for a moment, then sighed. "I'm not saying that good marriages are impossible. I just don't think they're guaranteed, and too many go down in the dust for my comfort."

It wasn't like she was interested in getting married again, either, so she didn't know why she felt so compelled to argue about this. She had her own reasons for not wanting to take those vows again.

"Fair enough, I guess," she said.

Colt's phone blipped, and he pulled it out of his back pocket and looked down at the screen. "It's the ranch cook. He needs to talk to me about something."

"Should I get Peg to show me where to start with cleaning things out, then?"

"Yeah, that would be the best," he said. "If you want me to carry anything in for you—"

"I'll be fine." She waved off his offer. "Go on and get back to work."

Colt headed toward the door, and Micha toddled after him, so Jane boosted up her toddler and kissed her plump cheek.

"You're staying with me," she said with a low laugh,

but she watched as the door shut behind Colt, then looked around at the silent kitchen.

She had no idea what was waiting for her here in Creekside. She was among family, but they were the people her late husband hadn't trusted.

She pulled her hair out of her face and heaved a sigh. *Father, guide me...* She didn't know what else to ask.

As Colt headed outside, the hot, grass-scented wind enveloped him and he felt the tension start to fade away.

Lord, keep me focused on my job, he prayed silently. *I don't know what Beau was thinking. If he was going to leave me the ranch, why complicate it on me? But she's Josh's wife, and I have no problem with sharing this with her... I just need Your help holding the ranch together. You know where the finances stand! The sooner this is resolved and Jane is on her way back to her life, the better. So smooth the road for that, Lord. And give me some grace in the meantime.*

There was a lot of work to get done that day, and he'd already used up a good chunk of it there at the lawyer's office. Beau hadn't been doing a lot of the day-to-day managing of the ranch anymore before he died, so the ranch hands already looked to Colt as the one to answer to. But he wasn't just the ranch manager now, he was owner. He'd have to hold a meeting when he told everyone together at the same time. If rumor didn't reach them first.

The main house was on the crest of a hill, and the dirt road that led toward the ranch hands' bunkhouse and canteen wound around the hill and toward the west where a patch of forest served as a backdrop for the low wooden buildings. The trees melted into some scrubby grassland beyond that served well in winter, giving the cattle the shelter of trees in the coldest weather, and some iron feeders and water troughs that were filled daily once the snow came. Now that it was summer, the cattle were enjoying the lush pasture farther east. Even in the summer months, Colt's mind skipped ahead to the next season. The work never eased up; it just changed form. That was ranch life.

His truck bounced over a pothole, and his vehicle rattled. The canteen and the bunkhouse weren't too far from the main house. When he arrived, he parked out front in his usual spot. A couple of work trucks were parked along the side, and he could hear the buzz of some male voice filtering out through the propped-open door. He pulled out his cell phone and dialed his mom's number in Wyoming. She'd moved out there five years ago, and it still felt strange to have her so far away. The Marshalls seemed to chase off anyone without a real good reason to stick around.

"Colt? That you, honey?" his mother said, picking up.

"Yeah. Hi, Mom."

"How's it going over there?" she asked. "Don't you have the reading of the will today?"

"Yeah. I just got back from it."

"And?" She sounded slightly breathless.

"And Beau came through. The ranch is mine."

"Yes!" His mother heaved a deep sigh. "I'm so glad. I was praying for this. You deserve that land, son."

Wasn't that the way…everyone praying for their own stake in something that didn't belong to them to begin with. It still felt wrong.

"There's a bit of a wrinkle, though," he said. "Josh's widow is here. Beau left her kids the cattle."

"He left them the—" his mother began. "What kids?"

"Josh had twins. He died before they were born. Two girls. And Beau left them the cattle."

"Josh had kids?" His mother paused for a couple of beats. "That egotistical jerk!"

"Josh?" Colt asked wryly.

"No, your uncle. Obviously. Even from the grave, he wants to ruin other people's happiness! He could have just left the ranch to you free and clear. Would that have been so hard? He didn't bother making up with Josh, so he was going to try and make up for that after the fact?"

"It was the right thing to do," he countered. "These are Josh's daughters, Mom. They look just like him."

"So give them something else. The cattle?" She was only getting started, he could tell.

"Mom, it's done," Colt said irritably. "And Beau's dead. There's no one left to be mad at."

"So Josh's widow is there?" his mother clarified.

"Yep. She's here. Just for a week or two while we sort out the paperwork and I get a loan to buy my cattle back."

"Your cattle. I like the sound of that. This was a long time coming, son, but I'm glad. I know you're a bit guilty right now, but trust me on this—you have nothing to feel guilty about."

He wished he felt as certain about that as his mother did.

"I just wanted to let you know what happened," he said. "I've got some stuff to take care of here, so I'd better let you go."

"All right. Back to work. I love you, son."

"Love you, too, Mom. Bye."

He hung up the phone and heaved a sigh. The family turmoil surrounding this inheritance wasn't quite so easy for him to dismiss. His mother was Sandra's sister, and she'd hated Beau. Beau had been the "idiot husband" who made her sister miserable. There hadn't been a lot of love lost between the two of them. But work called, and Colt didn't have the luxury of sitting around and beating himself up.

As Colt headed inside the canteen, his eyes took a moment to adjust after the bright sunlight.

"Hey, boss," a couple of cowboys said as he passed by a table where they were eating some wrapped sandwiches.

"Morning," he said, continuing on by.

Shawn, the ranch cook, was in the kitchen, wrapping up some hoagies in plastic wrap, and he turned when Colt came in, the door swinging shut behind him.

"You texted?" Colt said.

"Yeah." Shawn finished wrapping the sandwich in his hand and put it on the pile. "I know the timing isn't great, what with Mr. Marshall's passing, but I've got to give my notice."

"What?" Colt froze. "Don't tell me someone is paying you more—"

"Nah, my brother was in a bad accident in the city, and he's going to need my help running his drywalling business while he recovers. I said I'd come out, and I have no idea how long that'll take. Weeks? Months? No clue."

"I'm sorry about that," Colt said, his mind spinning ahead to job postings and interviews. "So…how much time will you give me?"

"I've got to leave in the morning," Shawn said.

"That soon!" Colt choked. "I don't have anyone to fill in. Are you sure you can't give me a few more days?"

"My brother has a big contract he has to complete, and his leg has been broken in two places. If I don't come, he'll have to break his contract and that will be costly. So I've got to get out there and lend a hand. I said that I would. I'm sorry, Colt. Ordinarily I'd give more notice. You know that. I'm not the kind of guy to just leave a place hanging."

"Yeah, I know that," Colt said with a sigh. "I'll figure it out. You've been loyal and reliable the last three years, and I'm glad to have worked with you. All the best to your brother on his recovery."

"Thanks."

"So…what do I need to know to keep this kitchen running?"

"I'm doing some wrapped sandwiches to stick in the fridge to get you through for a bit. I've got some frozen lasagnas ready to thaw and stick in the oven, and there's the burger fixings, too. That'll get you through a couple of dinners. The sandwiches are for pack lunches, and if you can cover breakfast—" He paused.

There would be meals to be served while Colt put out an ad for a cook. He was on a skeleton crew as it was… That had been Beau's way—and maybe that was just the way it had to be to keep this place above water. But there was one extra person on the ranch right now, and if she'd agree to pitch in for a day or two in the kitchen, and if Peg would watch the twins in the meantime, this might go a bit smoother. But whatever happened, he couldn't let Peg anywhere near that kitchen.

She meant well, but her cooking was terrible and the men would mutiny.

"That would be great," Colt said. "I'll figure out the rest. If you'd be so kind to stash as many sandwiches in the fridge as possible, I'll get your check cut for your last payout. I appreciate the time you've given us, Shawn. If you ever want to come back and work this ranch, the door is open."

They shook hands and Colt pushed down that rising anxiety as he headed for the door. He was the boss now—his work had only just begun.

Chapter Three

Jane came back inside the house carrying the last bag from the trunk of her car. She dropped it on the kitchen floor and wiped her forehead. The toddlers, who had been corralled by Peg for the few minutes it took for Jane carry in the bags, came shooting toward her with squeals of delight.

"Look at that!" Jane said, picking them both up. "I'm back!"

Every time she came back into the room, her daughters acted like it was the biggest event of their little lives. And maybe it was, but Jane loved it. Being a mom was both the hardest and the most satisfying role of her life.

Peg dished up some of the apple crisp onto a plate and slid it across the table in Jane's direction.

"You must be hungry," Peg said. "You've had a long day. I'll set to making some dinner, but in the meantime, eat that."

"Thanks." Jane looked down at the grayish mass on her plate. She looked up at the older woman and met with a pointed stare. She was expected to eat this, and while she was hungry, she wasn't sure she wanted to. She put the toddlers back onto the floor, closed her eyes and said a quick blessing before she picked up a fork and took a bite. The crisp was tasteless and slightly gluey. Jane swallowed with difficulty.

"I never had kids, but I do know that a mother has to eat on her feet or not at all," Peg said.

"That's the truth," Jane said with a smile. "Those two keep me hopping."

Peg leaned back against the counter. "So what do you do for a living, then?"

"I worked for a maid service," Jane said, grateful for an excuse to put her fork down.

"And just took the time off to come out here?" Peg pressed, raising an eyebrow.

"I—" Jane cast about, looking for a way to avoid revealing her financial situation, but it didn't seem possible. "I'm going to tell you the truth, Peg, because it's easier than trying to avoid talking about it. I lost the house Josh and I bought together. I couldn't make the bills on my own, and paying for day care is hard these days. I was balancing work with childcare costs, and trying to be here for my girls..." Tears pricked at her eyes, and she sucked in a deep breath. "I was laid off from my job at about the same time I sold the house. I didn't have a whole lot to lose by coming out here."

"What were you hoping to find here in Montana?" Peg asked quietly.

"I don't even know," Jane admitted.

"So you're looking to be supported," Peg concluded. "In memory of Josh."

"No." Irritation boiled up inside her. "I was looking for God's leading in the next step of my life. This is a time of transition—and I'm not here looking for handouts. As soon as we get this inheritance sorted out, I'll stand by my word and leave."

"And the cattle—you'll sell them back to Colt?" Peg asked.

"That's the plan," she replied. "What use do I have for cattle?"

"And the girls—" Peg said. "What about their inheritance?"

"I haven't had long to think about it, but I always did want to buy a house and start a bed-and-breakfast," Jane said. "It might work well with their inheritance, because when my girls are grown, their inheritance will have grown, too. It'll be secure in the value of the land. I have no intention of nabbing their money and making off with it. I want to build a life for them."

Peg eyed her for a moment, then nodded and said, "Smart."

"Thank you." Jane picked up the fork again and took another bite. No matter how it tasted, she needed to eat.

"There are women who go for all they can get," Peg said. "I was never one of them."

The inheritance… Peg hadn't been named in the will. Was she going to suffer because of Jane's daughters being remembered?

"Your brother's ranch—" Jane began.

Peg waved her off. "My late husband left me money. I'm fine."

"Oh…" That made Jane feel a bit better. "So what women are you talking about?"

Before Peg could answer, the side door opened and Peg turned away again. Colt came back inside, taking off his cowboy hat as he crossed the threshold.

"Hey," Colt said. "So, the cook quit."

"What?" Peg whirled around. "No notice? You can't stand for that!"

"His brother was in a bad accident. He's got to go help him out with his business. It's understandable," Colt replied.

"What will you do?" Jane asked.

"Well…" Colt rubbed his hand through his dark hair, his gaze flickering toward his aunt uncertainly. "I'm going to post a notice that we need a cook ASAP, and… we'll have to cover until then."

"You mean, you want one of us to cover in the kitchen until then," Peg retorted.

Jane raised an eyebrow and met Colt's gaze.

"We've got twenty ranch hands who live on premises," Colt said, turning to Jane. "We run a canteen to feed them, and until I can bring in another cook, I'm going to need some help out there."

"I'll do it. I'll do it," Peg muttered.

Colt shot Jane a grimace. "Actually, Peg, I was going to see if Jane would help me out in the kitchen. I mean, if she'd be willing to do it. And if you might be willing to watch the babies for a few hours a day."

He looked over at Jane again, and she could see the pleading in his eyes.

"I don't know," Jane said. "I mean, the girls are used to day care, but they don't know Peg yet, and—" Why not just have Peg do it? That's what she was wondering but didn't quite want to say.

"Could we talk outside?" Colt asked, hooking a thumb over his shoulder.

Jane pushed herself to her feet and followed him to the side door. Peg's sharp gaze seemed to dig into a spot between her shoulder blades and they stepped outside. Colt closed the door firmly after them.

"They'll quit on me, Jane," he said seriously as the door shut. "My aunt is a terrible cook. I'd have a mutiny on my hands, and I've got some well-trained ranch hands who are in demand. They'd walk on me, and I'm on a skeleton crew as it is. I can't afford to lose them."

"Is she that bad?" Jane asked with a short laugh.

Colt's expression remained grim. "Yes."

"How do you know I can cook?" she countered.

"I don't. I'm hoping you're better than Peg." He smiled slightly. "Are you?"

"I'm not bad," she replied. In fact, she was good enough that she felt confident in opening that bed-and-breakfast, but she wasn't here to start any new family feuds. "I hold my own. But Peg has already agreed to do it, and I don't see how you're going to get out of that without hurting her feelings. And who's to say she even wants to babysit two little live wires? My girls are sweethearts, but they know when they outnumber someone."

"Leave that to me," Colt said. "It wouldn't be for more than a day or two, until I get someone else in there. That's what it's like on a ranch like this one—we're a small outfit, and the profit margin is slim. We pitch in. Granted, I don't normally impose on guests, but I figure you're family, so…"

Jane smiled at that. "Well, you'll have to smooth it over with Peg."

"Her bark is worse than her bite," he replied, catching her eye, and he smiled in a way that made his eyes warm. "I can promise you that."

"Is it?" Jane asked with a low laugh.

He shrugged. "You'll have to take my word for it. She's a teddy bear if you know how to talk to her."

He brushed past her, his hand lingering on her shoulder, then he headed back up the steps, opening the side door again. "Peg?"

This Jane had to see, so she followed him inside. Peg had filled a sink with water and was about to start washing dishes. She looked up as they came in, raising her eyebrows, but staying silent.

"I was hoping you could do me a favor," Colt said.

"Besides cooking for the men?" she retorted. "That's ambitious of you."

"Jane's willing to cook down at the canteen, and I'm just thinking about your knee. It was pretty bad last month, and I don't want to make it worse."

"It's fine, now," Peg interjected.

"Yeah, but still. Jane's willing to cook for a day or two until I hire someone. I'll show her the ropes, and pitch in where I can. But I was hoping you could watch the girls, and at the same time help me in the hiring process. You can see right through someone's lies and garbage, and I need that. If you could stay here, watch the babies for Jane, and I could bring any possible hires by you…"

Peg softened, and she dried her hands then put them on Colt's shoulders.

"I've said it for years, Colt, and I'll say it again. You're a good rancher. You've got good instincts."

"A second opinion with a new hire never hurt," Colt replied. "I might have good instincts, but you've got the experience. What do you say?"

"If Jane's okay with it, I am," Peg said.

Colt gave Peg a grin. "Thank you." Then he turned

back toward Jane. "I'll bring you out there first thing in the morning. It's an early start—four a.m."

There was no apology in his voice for the early start.

"Sure." Jane looked over at Peg. "The girls always sleep in until seven. Will that be okay with you?"

Peg shrugged. "I might not have had children of my own, but I'll be fine. Give me your cell phone number in case I need you, but I don't anticipate a problem."

Jane would be pitching in. The last thing she wanted was to be remembered as the freeloader after she left. She'd help where she could, contribute where Colt asked, and when she did leave she could do so with her head held high. She wasn't a charity case, no matter how tenuous her current situation. God was providing.

The day slipped by, the girls keeping Jane busy as she fed them, changed them, took them outside to play, gave them some supper then bathed them together in the bathtub.

Peg made dinner that night—dry meatloaf, mashed potatoes that had been smashed into a virtual soup— and when the girls had been bathed, Peg headed out to the store for more milk and some bread. Honestly, Jane thought that Peg was making a run for it in order to get a few minutes to herself, and Jane didn't blame her a bit. Two toddlers were precious, but they over-ran everything.

"You look tired," Jane said, shooting Colt a smile.

"I always look tired," he replied with a low laugh. "But it's been a busy day. I posted the ad for a cook, so I'm praying for a quick reply."

"Is it always this hectic?" she asked. "I mean when something goes wrong."

"Yeah. Well, it wouldn't be if I had more manpower around here, but I don't dare hire extra employees beyond what we've currently got until I've done the math. Beau was a lot of things, but he was also good with numbers."

"That's understandable," she said. "But with Beau gone…isn't that one less person working?"

"Beau had left most of the running of the place to me," Colt replied with a shake of his head. "He took care of the finances, though, and this place is mortgaged up to the hilt. So I'm going to trust his choices for the time being."

Micha dropped the Cheerios she'd been munching on and started to whimper, and Jane scooped her up. She rooted through the diaper bag and pulled out a couple of formula powder packets. It took only a few minutes with Micha on her hip for Jane to shake up two bottles. It was almost bedtime, and the girls would be just wiped after so much excitement today. As if on cue, Suzie started to whimper, too, so Jane headed in the direction of the living room and sank onto the faded old couch.

"Come on, Suzie," she called.

Suzie stood in the kitchen, stubbornly refusing to come. Jane glanced around and realized she'd left the other bottle on the counter in the kitchen. She sighed—it had been a long day.

"Would you pass me the bottle?" she called to Colt in the kitchen. "Suzie is going to want it."

"Oh…yeah…" Colt scooped up the bag, held it open and perused the contents, then pulled out the bottle. Suzie clutched at Colt's leg and let out a wail. Micha started crying again—that little grizzle of tiredness— and Jane felt a wave of exhaustion of her own. Nothing was easy with twins, and a strange setting would only make this harder.

"Actually, could you just pick her up?" Jane asked hopefully.

Colt looked around himself, as if searching for an escape, then down at Suzie. Suzie fixed her big brown eyes on him, her lower tip trembling, and Colt bent down and lifted her up.

"Hello," Colt said softly.

"Bubba," Suzie whimpered.

"Her bottle," Jane translated. "They're both tired enough that they'll knock out pretty quickly with a bottle and a snuggle."

Colt handed Suzie her bottle, and she popped it into her mouth and leaned her head against Colt's shoulder. Those dewy brown eyes had a way of melting pretty much any heart, and Jane smiled over at him.

"Do you mind?" she asked.

"I guess not," Colt replied, and he sank into the easy chair across from her, the toddler in his arms. He adjusted Suzie on his lap and she let out a soft sigh, sucking away on her bottle as her eyes drooped. It felt odd to see her daughter in a man's arms. Jane had been on her own from the very beginning with her children, and yet she'd imagined what it would be like for Josh to hold them—to lend a hand when she was overwhelmed—countless times. A dad… Her girls didn't know what they were missing out on, did they?

She didn't, either, for that matter. Because as sweet as it would be to have some support, she wasn't willing to commit again. She sighed, dropping her gaze to the toddler in her lap.

Both girls were too old for their "bubbas" as they

called them. But Jane was a single mom, and with the two of them a bottle just helped the girls relax enough to sleep. She'd take all the help she could rustle up at bedtime, including this cowboy sitting across from her.

"Thanks," Jane said with a smile, and she looked down at Micha in her arms. Micha's eyes were shut, and a dribble of milk leaked out one corner of her mouth. They were still babies in so many ways—the bottles, the diapers, the chubby legs and cheeks...but they were growing up, too, and one of these days she'd have to put them into a day care again and she'd miss out on all of this.

"They do look like Josh," she said quietly. "I wanted my girls to look like me so badly. I imagined these identical little mini-mes running around, and—" Tears misted her eyes, and she blinked them back. "Considering that Josh didn't make it home, maybe I should be glad they look just like him."

Colt's dark gaze was locked on her, and when she met his eyes, he cleared his throat.

"I'm sorry about what I said earlier," he explained. "About marriage. I wasn't meaning to undermine what you had with my cousin or anything like that."

"It's okay."

"I'm glad that Josh didn't get bitter watching the marriages around us," Colt said. "I mean, he wrote off the family, but he didn't write off marriage completely. I went the opposite direction."

Except that Jane and Josh hadn't been as happy as she liked people to believe. Maybe they would have been if they'd had a chance to grow their relationship before he got deployed... She'd done her best. She'd Skyped with him, stayed cheerful for him, sent him packages, and when he came home on leave, she refused to fight with him. Even when he was being a jerk and pushing her to the limit. Because she only had a couple of weeks, and then he'd be gone again. It had been so much work, and she'd been so incredibly tired that when she found out she was pregnant after his visit home, the first thing she did was sit down and cry. Then she'd had to toughen up, because she couldn't let Josh see her crumbling when she Skyped with him that night and told him the news. He needed to focus on staying safe over there and coming back to be a daddy. It had taken every last ounce of her emotional strength.

Jane cast Colt a wan smile.

"No worries," she said. "I'll let some other woman talk you into the walk down the aisle."

Colt smiled wryly in return. "Peg's life goal, these days."

Colt didn't want marriage, but to be fair neither did she. Not again. Marriage had turned out to be so much more work than she'd ever imagined, and all she wanted was to raise her daughters. If she could open that bed-and-breakfast, then she'd be able to raise her girls and make an income at the same time. It would be the best of both worlds, and a huge amount of work. She knew that, but even so, it felt like less work than her marriage had been.

Maybe she and Colt had more in common than she thought, because while Jane believed in marriage, one was all her heart could take.

Colt looked down at the sleeping toddler on his lap. Suzie's red lashes brushed her ivory cheeks, and while her bottle was already on a side table next to him, she still made little sucking noises with her pursed pink lips. Josh's daughters were his, what…first cousins once removed? How did that relationship work? He wasn't sure—but they were part of his family and he felt a little tug of familiar recognition looking at them. They belonged in this zoo—in some way.

Colt didn't feel entirely comfortable with the way his heart softened just a little bit around this woman. Her silken long dark hair drew his gaze as she tucked it behind her ear. She was beautiful, but it was more than that. She was gentle, feminine…attractive in a way that tugged at him. But she was the kind of woman who ended up deeply disappointed in what he could offer. He'd been down this road before.

He cleared his throat and looked away. Maybe he was just lonely, and if that was the case he'd better learn to get used to it. Because this was Josh's family, and that made things a little harder to classify. He'd let Josh down already, and he felt an obligation toward his widow and daughters.

"I appreciate you being willing to help out with the canteen tomorrow," he said.

"I'm happy to help," she answered. "Josh used to talk about how much work a ranch was, and I can see what he meant."

"He talked about us," Colt said.

"From time to time."

"Good stuff or bad?" he asked with a wry smile.

"Do you really want to know?"

"Maybe not." Colt's arm was getting tired from holding Suzie in this position, and he lowered her down just a little more to make himself more comfortable. The toddler seemed to be asleep in his arms now, her breath coming long and deep, and it was oddly soothing to hold a sleeping baby. He'd never done this before. "So he really hated us, huh?"

"Josh—" Jane paused, then shrugged weakly. "He was hurt. I often thought that if he'd lived longer, he might have come back—made some peace with all of you."

"So why did *you* come out here to see us?" he asked. "Knowing how he felt about us and all that."

"For my girls," she said simply. "They need family. And I don't have much. I was raised by an aunt who's already passed away. I have a few cousins—but we grew up in different states and none of us are close. Some of us found each other on Facebook and we chat a bit, share pictures of our kids, but it isn't the same as having a real family. And I guess—on my side I can't provide that. But on their father's side, the family that remains is still in the same area."

"So you didn't resent us as much as he did?" he asked.

"I think there are two sides to every story," she replied. "Maybe even three or four. For Josh, this was about feeling personally rejected by his father. I suppose with Beau gone, I was hoping that there might be room in the family for Josh's little girls. In some small way, at least."

"Yeah, but you never would have popped by for a visit if it weren't for the inheritance," he countered.

"Not yet at least," she conceded. "In all honesty, I would have emailed Beau again one of these days just to say hello, maybe email a couple of pictures of the girls. They deserved a grandpa. I'm sorry they never got to meet him. But I was…intimidated. I'll have to admit."

Colt was silent for a moment. "Don't be intimidated by us."

"Peg's terrifying," she replied, but he could see the humor sparkling in her eyes.

"Don't be intimidated by me, then," he replied with a low laugh.

"I'll try," she said with a smile, and he was transfixed by just how beautiful she became when she smiled like that. He dropped his gaze.

She wanted family, and they did have that much out here. But in Colt's experience, family seemed to consist of a whole mess of relations letting each other down. Still, it was better than strangers doing the same.

Jane eased herself to her feet and tipped her cheek against the baby-soft curls on her daughter's head. "We can probably get them into bed now."

Colt rose to his feet, too, albeit a little less gracefully than Jane had. It was only a week or two, and then he'd have his privacy back. He could endure anything that long—even a beautiful houseguest.

They stopped at Jane's bedroom, and it was still bright—the summer sun still not having set for the night. Colt went inside first, pulling the curtains shut to dim it a little bit. It sported a double bed with plump pillows, a faded blue quilt on top and a rickety old dresser in one corner.

"This was Josh's room once upon a time." Colt glanced around the room. "It was cleared out after he left, though. Turned into a guest room."

Colt could hear the sting in his words—Josh had been erased from this house as quickly as Beau could make it happen. But that hadn't actually erased Josh from everyone's thoughts.

"Oh…" she breathed, and he could only guess at what she was feeling as she looked around the room once more. Jane pulled back the covers and laid her daughter on the bed. Micha stretched, then rolled over, still sleeping. Then she took Suzie from his arms, her cool hands brushing against the front of his shirt as she eased the toddler out of his grasp then laid Suzie next to her sister, their small chests rising and falling in a steady rhythm.

He couldn't lose focus here. Sure, Jane was pretty and vulnerable, sparking that male protective streak inside him. And sure, he'd missed out on a female presence around here—besides Peg for the last few days, but she was more like a tank in personality.

Colt cleared his throat. "Yeah, well… I'm going to be real busy around here, so after the canteen, you probably won't see a whole lot of me."

"Of course," she said. "I'm not here to be entertained. I'll pitch in where I can, and I'll be out of your hair as soon as we can sort out that paperwork."

"Thanks." He nodded curtly. "And…um…if you need anything…"

He looked around, spotted an old envelope on the dresser, pulled a nub of a pencil out of his pocket and jotted down his cell phone number.

"I'm sure I'll be fine," she said, but she accepted the envelope all the same.

"Jane, I feel like you deserve some warning." Colt crossed his arms over his chest and eyed her for a beat. "We're no Norman Rockwell family ideal out here. We are just regular people. Some of us are hurt. Personally, I'm a little messed up. We're trying really hard to overcome a whole lot of hurdles. We're a family, but are not always good at being one, either. If you're looking for everything these girls deserve, you should keep moving, because we'll never match up. Josh might have been onto something."

"I like to make up my own mind about people," she said quietly.

He threw her a quirky smile. "Don't say I didn't warn you."

Jane glanced toward the sleeping babies. "Noted. Don't worry about me, Colt. I can take care of my girls."

He nodded. "Okay, well... I've got some stuff to finish up tonight yet. Set your alarm for three forty-five."

She grimaced, and Colt laughed softly. "Yeah, that's ranch life for you. By the time you leave, you might be glad to see the back of us."

Chapter Four

Three forty-five was dark and cool. Jane turned off her cell phone alarm and looked over at her sleeping daughters. Their hair was mussed, their cheeks rosy from the warm night and Suzie's arm was flung over Micha's face in a position that Jane had learned to leave alone. It might not look comfortable, but they could sleep like that without any problem if they fell asleep on the floor at home. Her heart swelled with love whenever she watched them sleep.

This had been their father's bedroom—or so Colt had told her the evening before—and she felt a mist of tears at the thought of him. Marriage hadn't been easy with Josh, but that hadn't been his fault, either. A military life was a difficult one—soldiers put more than their lives on the line; their relationships were vulnerable, too. All that time apart, having to make up for it with just a few weeks together, and then all of the trauma Josh had to sort through that got in the way of him being able to really open up… It wasn't Josh's fault, but it had still been constantly difficult.

And here she was in Josh's childhood home—the

place he'd refused to come back to—and she was looking down at her own precious little girls. Was she making things more difficult for herself all over again by choosing to stay here for two weeks instead of going back and finding a place to rent?

Father, bless my children...

Jane prayed this prayer often, and she'd felt like this trip to their father's home ranch had been the right choice. Had she been too impulsive? It was possible. She hadn't exactly stopped to pray about it for very long. She'd just launched herself out here and trusted that God had been in the details. It had all *seemed* so providential at the time.

Jane got dressed quickly into a pair of jeans and an embroidered blouse, combed her hair and completely forwent any makeup. At this time of morning, she figured she could look just as exhausted as she wanted. She smothered a yawn and picked up her cell phone off the dresser. Some footsteps creaked down the hallway, and when she opened the door she saw Peg in a white terry cloth bathrobe that was cinched at the waist. She carried a Bible under one arm.

"Good morning," Peg said quietly.

"Do you always get up this early?" Jane asked as she stepped out of the bedroom.

"I like having the kitchen to myself for morning devotions, and this seemed like a good way," Peg replied.

"It'll do the job," Jane said.

"You'd better hurry. Colt will already be in the kitchen ready to go."

"Oh…" Jane looked back at her sleeping daughters one last time as she tucked her cell phone into her back pocket. "I'd better get moving then. Thank you for watching the girls for me. They'll sleep until seven. Maybe longer since yesterday was a big day. They're pretty easy to please for breakfast, and—"

"I'll be fine," Peg interrupted. "I won't be shy about calling you if I need to. I promise."

Jane cast the older woman a smile. "Thank you."

She headed down the hallway toward the kitchen, following the faint scent of brewed coffee. Colt stood by the counter, a mug in one hand and his hat on the counter next to him. He wordlessly slid a mug of coffee down the counter toward a carton of cream and a bowl of sugar.

"Thanks," she said, stifling another yawn. She put double the sugar into the coffee than she normally did, and a generous portion of cream to cool it down. She'd need more than caffeine this morning. Then she took a sip. It was the perfect temperature.

"How'd you sleep?" Colt asked.

"Surprisingly well," she said.

"Good, because this morning is going to be busy. Breakfast is always the same—oatmeal, eggs, bacon, toast and sometimes we'll put some corn bread on the menu, but not this morning. I figured we should keep this as simple as possible."

Jane gulped back her coffee, then put it down on the counter. "I'm ready."

"No breakfast?" he asked.

"Too early." She winced. "I'll eat later."

The sooner they fed the ranch hands, the sooner she could get back to her daughters.

"Great." He grabbed her mug and put them both into the sink. "The men will be eating by five thirty when the sun comes up. They'll arrive hungry. They're already doing one round of chores."

Hard work—wasn't that what Josh had always told her? A ranch was about blood and sweat, and in Josh's opinion there was very little payoff. But Jane was seeing a different side to this ranch—when someone invested blood and sweat because they loved it. Colt was definitely a man who was here because there was nowhere else he'd rather be.

Colt opened the side door and waited for her to exit the house before he followed her, closing the door firmly behind him. Outside, the air was warm already and she could hear the soft chirp of crickets from the grass.

Colt led the way to his truck and he opened her door for her, then headed around the driver's side while she hopped up and slammed it shut. Colt started the truck and backed out.

"So, how long have you worked the ranch?" Jane asked.

"Ever since I was about fourteen," Colt replied. "My mom was working as the cook here at the ranch. She was Sandra's sister—I told you that, right? Well, Beau and Sandra gave her a job and she was just glad to have a safe place to raise me after my dad left. The cook normally lives in the bunkhouse with the other ranch hands, but because she had me, it was different. Plus, she was family. When I was a teenager, Mom decided I could use some responsibility. My uncle was willing to pay me a pittance for a whole lot of work. It turned out to be a good combination."

"Lots of work and low pay?" she asked with a short laugh. "That was a good combination?"

"Yeah, I was a handful. I was getting involved with a

rough group of kids at school, and hard work combined with a very small income made me less available for getting into trouble, and meant I couldn't attract a whole lot of attention, either. It was actually pretty smart."

The truck bumped over the gravel drive that curved away from the house. She couldn't see too much—the moon was only a sliver and the headlights from the truck sliced a path in front of them along the road.

"Where is your mom now?" she asked.

"She went south to Wyoming. She took a job at a ranch out there when things got too tense with Beau."

This family did seem to have a lot of drama in its wake. "What happened? Do you mind if I ask?"

"My mom backed Josh when he said he wanted to join the army. Josh and I were both seventeen at the time, so we were just about adults. But the Marshalls can take something small and turn it into a huge mess. Mom and Beau started bickering a lot, and since Mom thought I had a chance at making a career for myself there with Beau, she decided it was better for her to go find another job and let me continue on." His expression grew clouded, then he shrugged it off. "So what about you? What does your family look like?"

"Small," she said. "I was a raised by a childless aunt. My mom died in a car accident when I was too young to remember. Her family was little, but also really fractured. There were no extended-family Christmases or anything like that. So I also harbored a few fantasies about a big extended family."

"The picturesque kind, I'm sure," he said, casting her a wry smile.

"Of course. What other kind is there?" she asked with a laugh. "We all have our fantasies, don't we?"

"I've let go of those," Colt replied. "It's easier that way."

They drove in silence for a couple more minutes until the road narrowed and slanted upward, the engine rumbling as they pulled up next to a long, low building. A few lights were on inside, but most of the windows were dark.

"That's the bunkhouse," Colt said, then he pulled forward again and passed the first building, parking in front of the second and turning off the engine. "And this is the canteen."

There wasn't much to see this time of the morning when everything was dark.

"Let's get in there. We've got a lot to do," Colt said.

Colt hopped out of the truck and Jane followed. He unlocked the front door of the building and opened it for her to go inside first. He flicked on an overhead light that blazed to life, making Jane blink. The main room was filled with tables and long benches. The front had a couple of tables, one of which had big hot-water and coffee canisters. Colt strode down the main aisle between the tables and led her past swinging doors into the kitchen. He flicked lights on there, too.

"Hair net," he said, pointing to a box on the counter.

Jane took one and bundled her thick, dark hair up into it—as much as would fit, anyway. He sent her a rueful smile. "Cute."

"Shut up," she chuckled. "You'd better put one on, too."

Colt pulled a clean bandana out of his pocket and tied it around his head. "This works, too."

They both washed their hands at the sink, then Colt opened a cupboard and pulled out a large pot.

"The oatmeal is down there," he said, pointing at another cupboard. "The last cook left some frozen lasagnas to thaw in the fridge. So we can do those for dinner tonight. I'm going to pull out some wrapped sandwiches for bagged lunches."

Colt was focused and brisk in his movements. He was just so…strong. It was hard to pull her gaze away from him. This family sure had some good-looking men. Was that bad to notice? Jane watched him for a moment, feeling a vague sense of misgiving. What was she even doing out here? She certainly wasn't feeling like she fit in right now. Had this really been God's leading, or her own wishful fantasies?

She sighed and bent down to pull out a large box of dry oatmeal. She could measure water and oats like anyone else. She'd add some sugar to the oats while they cooked, too, and a bit of nutmeg. That's how she made it at home.

The pot that Colt had deposited on the counter was massive, and she rooted around until she found a large measuring cup, then set to work.

"How many of these will we need?" she asked, holding up a four-cup measurer filled with oats.

"Six," he said. "Then double that for water."

"Right." She eyed Colt again, watching him as he flicked open a lunch bag and tossed in a sandwich, an apple, a bag of chips, a muffin…

She turned back to the pot and started to measure in the oatmeal and water.

"Colt," she said, turning toward him again.

"Yeah?"

"Are you happy?"

Colt folded shut a lunch bag and eyed her speculatively. "Why?"

"I'm curious. Does this life make you happy?"

"I guess," he replied. "Right now, this life is stressing me out."

She smiled at his dry humor. "If you could do anything, and money wasn't a problem, what would you do?"

"This—with more workers," he replied with a shrug. "Being that close to the line financially all the time tends to suck the joy out of the work."

"Hmm." She slid the heavy pot onto a burner and turned it on. She could empathize with that. Too much pressure on anything could ruin it—she'd learned that with her marriage to Josh.

"What about you?" he asked. "If money weren't a problem…"

"I'd build a business of my own," she said. "I'd buy a house—big enough to turn into a bed and breakfast—and I'd set up my life so that I could be completely self-sufficient. It would be a simple life, but mine. Only mine. You know?"

Colt's gaze was riveted to her as she spoke, then he nodded slowly. "Yup. I get it."

"People try to set up the single mom a lot," she said with a short laugh. "They toss any man with a pulse in my direction. Doesn't matter if we'd have nothing in common—if he's single, they're going to suggest him."

"You obviously aren't interested," he said.

"I'm not. All I want is a life of my own. No husband. No other pressure. No constant trying, trying, trying to keep a relationship alive. I just want…something easy.

I want to worry about raising two girls and building a career that will provide for us. And that's it."

She was saying too much, and she clamped her lips shut. What did this man care about her yearning for some financial freedom?

"Yeah, I get that, too," Colt said, resuming the lunch preparation again. "And I've got a bit of family around, but mostly it's the Marshalls. In a town this size, you get pulled in whether you're a blood relative or not, so there's a lot of friends of Josh's cousins and the like who get tossed in my direction. It's hard for people to understand when someone doesn't want to get married. They think you just haven't met the right one."

"I did meet the right one," she said. "And our marriage was short, but I'm ready to just be alone."

"I'm the one guy who can understand that."

Yes, he was, wasn't he? They might have different views of the value of marriage, but they both agreed on their desire to avoid it.

They exchanged a look, and Jane laughed softly. "I'll make a deal with you, Colt Hardin. We'll never try to set each other up, and if there are any big family gatherings, we'll sit together so we have someone to talk to without any pressure."

"I just avoid the big family gatherings, but your idea isn't bad," he said with a chuckle.

"We might end up friends yet, Colt," she said, pulling a long-handled spoon from a drawer and giving the pot a stir.

Colt didn't answer, but when she looked over her shoulder, she saw him tossing an apple into a lunch bag, a smile tugging at the corners of his lips. He glanced up, met her gaze and she saw the sparkle of humor in his dark eyes.

"Turn up the heat, or that pot will take a year to boil," he said.

Yes, they might end up friends yet. She'd been longing for a family, and she couldn't exactly be choosy. These were her daughter's relatives, and she'd make the best of it.

Colt could feel her eyes on him as he turned back to packing the last of the bag lunches. She made him feel uncomfortably aware of her presence in the kitchen—the soft tink of the spoon against the side of the pot as she dipped it in for a quick stir, the softness of her pale hand as she tucked away a stray tendril of dark hair. Even in that ridiculous hair net she looked beautiful. Was it okay to notice that if they were both agreed on their unwillingness to get into a relationship?

It was a relief to know that she wasn't looking for marriage, either. It took the pressure off. He was so used to fending off the advances of single women in Creekside that it was oddly liberating to be standing in the kitchen with a woman he didn't have to disappoint.

He folded the last lunch bag and lined them up in a tray. He should go—she could take care of the rest. That was why she was here in this kitchen, after all, to free him up to do his own work.

"Okay, I should—" he started.

"Oh! It's boiling!" Jane interjected. "I need a longer spoon than this. Is there one?"

"Yeah, hold on," Colt said.

Colt crossed the kitchen and pulled open a drawer

that had ladles and serving spoons, but not what he was looking for.

"Hold this," Jane said, handing him her current spoon and pulling open the drawer next to the one he'd been looking in. She was right—that's where they were.

"Is this bigger?" She held one up. "Nope."

Back into the drawer she went, and Colt stood there watching her. He wasn't supposed to be hanging out in the kitchen with this beautiful interloper.

"Here we go," she said, and she held up a wooden spoon with a longer handle. "This will work. Sorry, you probably didn't need to hold that."

Colt laughed softly and dropped it into the sink. "You sure you'll be okay here?"

"I'll sort it out," she replied with a shrug.

Outside the kitchen window, it was still dark. He couldn't make out any details, since most of what he could see was the kitchen reflected back at him. But across the gravel parking area he could see a couple more lights come on in the bunk house, piercing through his own reflection.

"If you need anything, you can call me on my cell," he said. "The guys are nothing to worry about. They'll eat up and go."

"Okay." She glanced over, smiled.

"Okay," he repeated, then cleared his throat. "I'll... um...see you later, then."

"Yep. See you."

Colt headed back over to the tray of packed lunches and picked it up. It wasn't heavy so much as awkward, and he balanced it with both hands as he headed out the swinging door to the side table where those bagged lunches always waited. He set down the tray and glanced over his shoulder once more toward that kitchen door that was still swinging its way back to a resting position. It would be easier to dismiss her if she weren't quite so attractive. And he didn't mean that in a strictly physical sense, either. Because she was definitely pretty, but she was the kind of woman who made him want to hang around and hold spoons if that was what it took to spend a few more minutes with her. He'd have to practice a whole lot more self-control than this.

Work was waiting. He'd leave her to her job and get to his.

The day was a busy one, and by noon, Colt had three responses to his online posting for a cook. That was a quick turnaround, and he was grateful for it. Two of the applicants had only minor cooking experience, but the third had all the qualifications he was looking for. Colt gave him a call and asked him in for an interview at three.

Paul Vich was an older guy, dressed neatly with a bristly gray mustache. He came up the drive in an old Ford ten minutes early. Colt drove him down to the canteen for the interview in his ranch truck, leaving Paul's truck parked up by the house. The dining room was empty, and when he glanced into the kitchen, Jane was there and the lasagnas were out of the fridge and on the counter. He paused and watched her through the glass window in the door for a moment. She was fiddling with the stove settings, it seemed. He pushed the door open, and she glanced back.

"Hi," Jane said. "Checking up on me?"

"A little bit," he admitted. "I'm doing an interview for a cook."

"Oh, good. Because I'll do my best, but I don't normally cook for twenty..." She made a face, and Colt chuckled.

"We'll see how it goes. You okay, there?"

"I think so." She hit a button, opened the oven and stuck her hand inside, then nodded. "There we go. That was the oven this time."

She was handy. Was that even something a woman wanted to hear? But she seemed to take on a challenge without too much fuss, and that was a quality that Colt was forced to admire. He'd half expected Jane to be a bit helpless—widowed, mother of twins, overworked and needing a break somewhere—but she wasn't and he realized he liked that. She was not just an extra responsibility around here—she was actually helping out, and right now that took a load off his shoulders.

Colt went back into the dining room where Paul was waiting. Colt sat down and went over the résumé with him, asking him some questions about his certifications and cooking experience. He was calm and collected, answered all the questions after a brief pause and a furrowing of his brow.

"We need someone who could start right away," Colt said. "When are you available?"

"I could start tomorrow."

"It's a live-in position. That a problem for you?"

"Nope. I could do that."

Too good to be true? Colt wasn't sure. He didn't know this fellow from Adam, and for all he knew the résumé might be a complete fabrication. But he didn't have a lot of time to be picky, either. He'd check his references, but he wanted Peg's opinion, too.

"There is one more person I'd like you to meet," Colt

said, and he pulled out his phone and tapped in a text then pressed Send.

"The current cook?" Paul asked, raising his eyebrows.

"No, she's just standing in," Colt replied, glancing back toward the kitchen. "Let's head back to the house."

This was where Colt needed Peg's insights. She'd never been stingy with her opinions before, and he'd be glad for them today. He got a return text and glanced down at it. Peg was at the house, as he'd been relatively certain she would be, considering that Jane was here in the canteen.

Colt drove Paul back up the winding drive, and Paul made small talk as they went. Colt learned that Paul was widowed and had two married daughters. He currently lived in town with one of them.

"You sure a live-in job is going to work for you?" Colt asked him as they hopped out.

"I'll be level with you," Paul replied. "I love my girls and I love those grandbabies, but I miss horses and cattle and some quiet in the mornings. I think my daughter's marriage could use a bit of space, too, truth be told."

"Oh, yeah?"

"They need time alone. That's all. And having me kicking around isn't helping. A live-in position would give me an excellent excuse to get out from underfoot. I'm supposed to be retired, but I'd rather work another couple of years yet. I'm not worn out yet."

"That makes sense," Colt admitted. "Come on inside."

Colt parked in his regular spot and hopped out. Paul followed him to the side door, and they went inside together. The kitchen was empty, but he could hear a toddler's wail coming from deeper inside the house. Peg had her hands full this afternoon, it would seem. A patter of little feet came through the living room, and one of the toddlers ran at full speed into the kitchen, a new diaper clutched in one hand and a beaming smile on her face. She lurched to a stop when she saw the men, looked between them for a beat, then launched herself at Colt with a squeal.

Colt didn't have much choice but to bend down and scoop her up, or she'd have collided with his dusty jeans. The toddler squirmed around and reached for his hat with one pudgy hand.

"Hey, there," Colt said to the girl. "Where's your sister?"

The wailing from the other side of the house stopped, and Colt looked over at Paul and shrugged. "Kids, right?"

"Don't I know it. I've got a grandson a little younger than this one, and a granddaughter a little older. But they keep you busy."

The girl managed to get a hold of his hat at that point, and Colt took it off and dropped it on her head. It covered her face completely, and he could hear the hollow echo of her giggle from inside. He pulled it up so he could see her face, and she giggled again. Man, this kid was cute. And he still couldn't tell if it was Suzie or Micha. If Jane were here, she'd clue him in.

"Again!" the toddler squealed, pulling the hat down. Colt chuckled, and then the second toddler erupted into the kitchen, Peg a few steps behind.

"How old are they?" Paul asked.

"Two," Colt replied. That was one thing he was certain about.

"Enjoy this. They grow up and get married faster than you'd think," Paul said with a chuckle.

Colt realized that Paul was assuming the girls were his, and he was about to correct him when Peg came forward with a smile.

"I'm Peg Melton," she said, and she shook Paul's hand firmly. "So you're here about the cook position?"

"Yes, ma'am." Paul pulled off his hat and tucked it under his arm.

"I'm going to cut right to the chase here," Peg said, narrowing her eyes. "You're older than we usually get applying. Why aren't you retired on a porch?"

"Retired?" Paul eyed Peg for a moment, and Colt could see them both sizing the other up. "I could ask you the same thing."

"I'm needed," she retorted.

"Well, I'm not needed," he said with a shrug. "I was retired. I sold my house and put my money in with my daughter and her husband for a nice big house we could all live in together. Turns out, I'm underfoot. So I've decided to put off my retirement for a stretch and give my daughter some space."

"Where'd you come from?" she asked.

"Originally? Venton. Two hours west. My daughter's husband was a schoolteacher out there, but he just transferred to Creekside High last September."

"Ah." Peg chewed the side of her cheek. "You're not married?"

"Does it matter?" Paul's brows rose.

It was actually an illegal question, and Colt needed

to put a stop to this right quick. "No, it doesn't," he said quickly. "That's not something we can even ask."

Paul didn't take his eyes off Peg, but a small smile came to his lips. "I'm widowed."

"Were you happy?" she asked softly.

"Peg, this is *way* off track here," Colt said, and at that moment, the other toddler started tugging on his pants. At a loss of what to do, he bent down and scooped her up, too, so that he had both girls in his arms as he shot a blazing look at Peg. The last thing he needed was to be sued for unprofessional hiring practices.

"I was real happy," Paul replied. "And I hope my daughters have as much happiness as I did. But sometimes in the beginning there are some bumps before you get there."

"I'd agree with that," Peg said with a nod. "Who cooked in your home?"

"Me," Paul replied with a shrug. "When I had time. I liked it. She hated cooking."

Colt looked helplessly down at the toddlers. The second little girl had found his shirt pocket and was pushing a damp little hand down into it.

"Are you a Christian, Paul?" Peg asked after a beat of silence.

"Peg, we are so far past legal here, it isn't even funny!" Colt exploded.

"Yes, ma'am, I am," Paul said with a low laugh. "If that sets your mind at ease, at all."

"Hmm." Peg didn't look convinced.

"Okay, we're done here," Colt said, and he tipped both toddlers at once into Peg's arms, plucking his hat out of the one toddler's sticky grasp. She squished up her face, her eyes welling with tears, and on instinct Colt bent down and kissed the top of her head.

"Sorry, kid," he whispered. "I need that. I look dumb without a hat."

Then he turned and strode back to the front door, pulling it open.

"Thank you for coming by, Paul," Peg said.

"Yeah, thank you," Colt added, then gritted his teeth in annoyance. He'd figured Peg would have been more discreet than that. "I've got your number here. I'll give you a call."

Colt shook Paul's hand, and the older man left. As Colt closed the door he turned back to the older woman with an exasperated look.

"What was that?" he demanded.

"He'll do," she replied calmly. "Go ahead and hire him."

"You can't ask someone about their marital status and their religious affiliation in an interview, Peg!"

"I don't know him, though," she replied with a shrug. "Anyone from around here, I'd know that already."

"Okay, so what makes him acceptable?" Colt asked irritably. "Out of curiosity."

"He cooked for his family," she replied with a curt nod.

"That was the part you liked?" he asked.

"It shows that he loves to cook—he's obviously good at it, or his wife would have taken back the chore in a heartbeat. Trust me on that. And, he's not the type of man to bow to male pressure. In our generation, a man who cooked would get some ribbing. So if he stood up for that because it worked for his marriage, then he's got some character. We need character."

Colt rubbed his hand over his face. "Okay." He had to grudgingly admit that she had some logic behind all that illegal questioning. "Well, thanks."

"So go on and hire him," she said. "You need a cook, and he'll do fine." She looked down at the toddlers in her arms. "And these two need a snack."

Colt picked up his phone and looked down at the résumé in his hand. After his aunt had trampled every legal boundary imaginable, he'd better hire this guy or he could face a lawsuit.

And next time he had to hire someone, he wouldn't be asking his aunt's input. His own instincts and a few reference checks would have to be enough from now on.

"Cat!" one of the toddlers hollered, and he looked back to see a little girl leaning out of Peg's arms and stretching toward him.

Cat. It sounded like that was what she was calling him. It might be as close to Colt as that little mouth could manage.

"I'll be back, kiddo," he said, and he gave the toddler his most reassuring grin.

What was he doing? He'd been right irritated with Peg today, but he'd also enjoyed this... What could he say? There was something about these rambunctious little girls in his home that warmed the place up. And it was kind of nice to have little hands reaching for him like that. He'd never entertained the thought of having kids of his own, but he could see why guys wanted the family life. It was sweet...when it worked out.

He'd been through a few breakups already, though. Women wanted a man willing to talk about marriage and kids—and he hadn't been that guy. He'd always kept his heart pretty securely protected.

Getting used to this, and then having it torn apart when the relationship went bust would be more heartbreak than he even wanted to think about. There was a reason why he was cautious with women.

Whatever—this was a short-term thing. And their mother would be back in a few hours. He was just the guy with the hat and the front shirt pocket. He was entirely replaceable.

Chapter Five

Jane leaned against the doorjamb, looking out the cracked kitchen door as the men lined up to take another serving of lasagna. Hats were off, their hair mussed up and their exposed forearms were bronzed from the sun. They were laughing and talking—deep voices reverberating against the dining room walls.

All she'd done was bake the lasagna, but she still felt a surge of satisfaction to see the men eating heartily. She'd made the salad to go on the side, and the garlic toast. It hadn't exactly been taxing. She hadn't thought of getting a plate for herself, but now that she was smelling the food and watching the men power through it, she wished she'd thought of it.

She let the door swing shut again and turned to survey the mess. She headed for the dishwasher. She could start with a few dishes, at least.

Her phone pinged, and she glanced down at it. Peg had sent her a picture of the girls eating macaroni and cheese—cheese up the eyebrows on both of them. She smiled, then typed in a reply—Adorable! I'm hurrying to clean up, and then I'll be back.

Peg seemed to do better with the girls than Jane had anticipated. Jane had gone back to the house after breakfast, and only came back a few hours later to start dinner, and from what she could see the girls liked Peg. Peg softened up to be almost unrecognizable when she talked to them. Maybe there was some family recognition there, because all three of them seemed to be enjoying their time together. This was what she'd come for, wasn't it? She'd wanted her girls to be able to have family—and seeing pictures of them happily cared for by their great-aunt… Hopefully her girls would grow up with more family connection than she had.

The sound of cowboy boots on the kitchen floor made her turn, and she realized belatedly that she'd been hoping to see Colt. Instead, a gangly blond-haired cowboy sauntered into the kitchen. His jeans were dirty from a day of work, and he shoved a thumb into his belt loop, glancing around the kitchen.

"Evening," he said.

"Hi." She gave him a quick smile and tucked her phone back into her pocket. "Can I help you with something?"

"I heard we had a new cook."

"I'm very temporary," she said, turning back toward the sink and starting the water. "You'll have a proper cook soon enough."

"That was a good meal," he countered. "You should stick around."

"Thanks. But your last cook was the one who actually made it. I didn't do that much."

The cowboy crossed the kitchen and leaned against the counter next to her. He eyed her for a moment, his gaze moving over her in a way she didn't like.

"I'm Ross," he said. "Who are you?"

"I'm out of your league, Ross," she replied with a small smile. "And also busy."

Ross barked out a laugh. "A guy can still hope, can't he? You single?"

"Should it matter?" She raised an eyebrow. "I said I'm busy. You'd better get back to work."

"I have a few minutes," he said, settling in against the counter. "You're cute."

She sighed. This cowboy was at least five years younger than she was, and he likely didn't get around women too often working this ranch.

"Ross," she said pointedly. "I have to clean up. Please. Let me just finish up."

"You could take a little break," he said with a shrug. "Who'd know?"

"What part of 'I'm busy' don't you understand?" she snapped.

"You want to go out sometime?" he pressed. "I get an evening off tonight. I could take you into town. You ever been to the Burnt Barn?"

What was that? A bar? She didn't drink, and she didn't frequent bars, either, for that matter. It didn't actually matter. She ignored him and pulled open the dishwasher.

"You could probably use some fun," he went on. "Loosen up. Have a good time."

"No!" Jane sent him an annoyed look, her voice rising. "Look, buddy. I'm a single mom. I have two kids." She raised two fingers in case he needed the visual. "I'm not where *anyone* goes for a good time, okay? My fun days are well in the past. So do yourself a favor and find someone your own age."

Ross's jovial smile chilled, and he straightened. But before he could answer her, another pair of boots sounded behind them and Jane's stomach clenched. She could eventually get rid of one thick-skulled cowboy, but if she had to deal with more than one of them... She swallowed, sending up a quick prayer before she turned around.

This cowboy she knew, and she felt a wave of relief to see Colt saunter into the kitchen. He took his cowboy hat off and his dark gaze swept between them, an unimpressed look on his face.

"Evening, Ross," Colt said, his voice deep and loud. "Don't you have work to do?"

"Uh, yeah—" Ross glanced toward Jane once more, but that smile had returned. "If you change your mind, now—"

"Not going to happen," she said, giving him a tight smile of her own. "Have a good night."

Ross headed toward the kitchen door, but Colt shot out a hand and caught Ross by the shoulder.

"Wait," Colt said. "Can I have a word with you?"

"I just stopped in to say hello," Ross said quickly, but his tone was suddenly a whole lot more respectful.

"I heard her tell you real clear that she wasn't interested," Colt said, lowering his voice, but not low enough that Jane couldn't make out what he was saying. "And when a man hears those words, that's his cue to clear out. Did your old man never teach you that? It's called consent, and it goes for pretty much every interaction you have with a woman."

Color rose in Ross's face, and Jane dropped her gaze, almost feeling sorry for the guy. But not quite.

"Now, if she *wanted* to talk to you, that's another

story," Colt went on, his tone like iron. "If she wanted to go out with you, there's no law against that. But if she doesn't want to be talking to you—"

"Yeah, yeah, got it," Ross interrupted, and he made a move to keep walking, but Colt's hand was still firmly on his shoulder, holding him in place.

"That's strike one," Colt said, his voice so quiet that Jane almost didn't hear it. "I see anything like that again, and I write you up. This is a ranch where a woman can work or visit without having to fight off my ranch hands. Respect comes first. Your romantic life is the least of my concerns."

Colt released Ross's shoulder, and the smaller cowboy headed out of the kitchen without a backward glance.

"You embarrassed him," Jane said.

"He needed to hear it," Colt said curtly. "I'm not apologizing for how I run my own ranch."

"Fair enough."

"You okay?" he asked.

"He was annoying me, but I was this close to getting my message across," she said.

"Okay. Well, if that kind of thing happens again while you're here, you tell me and I'll do more than give warnings."

She nodded, because she was relieved that Colt had stepped in. Normally when a woman was wrangling two toddlers, it was an effective deterrent to any men in the area. But without the toddlers with her, she felt oddly exposed—she might even look available. And that couldn't be further from the truth.

"You want a hand in here?" Colt asked. "I figured

I could help you clean up. It would go faster with the two of us."

"Sure," Jane said. "Thanks."

Colt disappeared out that swinging kitchen door again, and Jane did feel better for his presence in the canteen. Colt was strong, confident and he seemed to have a firm hand on the running of this place. Maybe she could learn a few things from him for when she was running her own business, too. Except she wouldn't have a muscular cowboy on hand to fend off unwanted admirers for long. She'd have to find a way to discourage them that was easier than this. This wasn't the first time she'd had to fend off unwanted advances in the workplace, although when she'd been a maid she had been able to tell them that she'd be fired if she got socially involved with clients.

Colt came back through the swinging doors carrying a tray stacked with dirty dishes. He placed them on an island, and then brought a pile to the counter next to her.

"I've been thinking of putting my wedding ring back on," Jane said, accepting the plates with a nod of thanks.

"Yeah?" Colt said.

"It might discourage some of those guys if they assume I'm married," she said.

"It might," he agreed. "How come you haven't done it yet?"

Jane felt some heat rise in her face, and she turned her attention to rinsing the plates for a moment before she said, "Because it would be hard."

"Wearing Josh's ring?" Colt asked quietly. "The memories?"

"It would be a reminder of the husband I lost," she admitted. "But it would also be a reminder of a hard time. When I finally took that ring off two years ago it felt like a weight being lifted from my shoulders. I don't want you to think I didn't love Josh with my whole heart, because I did. But loving him was a lot of work, too. Standing by him. Supporting him from afar… All of it. It was work."

"Don't put the ring back on for us," Colt said. "I won't let anyone else bother you. Besides, I hired a cook this afternoon. He starts tomorrow."

Jane gave him a curious look. "That quickly?"

"I needed a cook," he said with a shrug.

Jane rinsed a plate and put it into the dishwasher. Colt joined her at the sink. They worked together for a few minutes in silence, loading up the plates and cups.

"I'm sorry marriage wasn't easier for you," Colt said, dropping a handful of cutlery into the appropriate slot.

"The problem wasn't Josh," she said. "I have to be honest about that. Josh was a good man dealing with some tough stuff."

"Well, I don't think the problem would have been you, either," he replied.

She shot him a small smile. "The problem was life, Colt. That's what marriage is—it's hard work. It takes a lot of energy and dedication, and I wouldn't undo a moment of my marriage to Josh. It was hard in a lot of ways, and it left me exhausted, but I loved him. And he gave me my beautiful girls. I just…don't want to do it again."

Was it terrible that after three years of marriage, she had already slipped out of the romantic honeymoon stage of things?

She looked down at her left hand in the suds—no rings. When she'd taken off her wedding ring after a year of mourning, she'd felt like herself again. Freer, calmer, lighter. Maybe it would seem heartless to anyone else looking in, but she didn't want to have to put that wedding ring back on. Maybe there would be another way to discourage unwanted advances—something she hadn't thought of yet. There was a lot of Biblical advice to married women, but not a whole lot for the single woman who wanted to stay that way.

Provide for me, Father, she prayed in her heart. *And for my girls. Show me how to be single again.*

Colt pulled open the passenger-side door of his truck for Jane, then headed around to the driver's side. The cleaning up hadn't taken too long with both of them working at it, and he'd enjoyed it more than he normally enjoyed cleaning up massive loads of dishes. There was something about Jane that made even the most mundane stuff into something special. It wasn't "fun" exactly, but he couldn't think of anything else he'd rather be doing, all the same. It was a small price to pay for a bit of time with her—something Ross had tried for, too.

He was still pretty upset with Ross, though. Colt had stopped outside the kitchen door and heard everything. If she'd shown any interest in Ross, Colt would have backed off and left the two of them alone to talk, but she hadn't. And if he was forced to get really honest with himself, he'd been glad of it.

Which was stupid, because the thing he and Jane had in common was a mutual desire to stay single. If she changed her mind, that wasn't his business. He knew where he stood, and that was what mattered.

When Colt got up into the driver's seat, Jane had already buckled her seat belt.

"I've got to drop my truck off at the garage," Colt said. "It's not far from the house. One of our guys is going to change the oil this evening. We've got a pretty strict schedule for the ranch vehicles. We can walk back to the house from there. It'll take like ten minutes."

"Oh, sure," Jane said. "Do what you have to do."

Jane looked down at her phone and smiled wistfully. When she felt his gaze on her, she held it up, revealing a photo of her twins eating what looked like mac and cheese.

"Cute," he said, turning the key.

"I miss them," she said. "Even when it's only been a few hours."

Colt backed the truck out and headed down the drive.

"I can't tell them apart," Colt said. "How do you do it?"

"Micha has a freckle on her forehead," Jane said. "That's all I've got. Physically, at least. Their personalities are very different. Micha's the leader. She'll be the first one to start trouble, and she was the first one to walk. Suzie's quieter. She's more of a thinker. She said *Mama* first."

"I'll have to look for the freckle," Colt chuckled. "I saw them when I stopped by to talk to my aunt about hiring the new cook. And they looked pretty happy, if that makes you feel any better."

"It does, actually."

The truck bumped over a pothole, and Jane's hand flew up to the window to stabilize herself.

"Sorry," he said. "We've got to fill that one in. Every time it rains it hollows out again."

He turned up the narrow road that led to the garage. It was shaded by a few trees, and he drove up to the front where the doors were open. Another truck was already in there, and Colt parked to the side. He looked over at Jane as he turned off the engine, and she pulled a hand through her dark hair, her face looking flushed from the heat of the day. He tossed the keys into the visor.

"We walk from here," he said. He wasn't supposed to be noticing how beautiful she was—at least not appreciating it quite this much. He wasn't like Ross—he knew the line and he respected it.

They both got out of the truck and slammed their doors behind them. It was almost seven, and while sunset was still a couple of hours off, the sunshine was warm and golden and the shadows stretched long. Colt started down the lane toward the road, and Jane fell into step beside him. He slowed his pace a little to make it easier for her to keep up. It felt good to have her company out here—just the two of them in the sunshine-scented air.

"So, Peg says that you're planning on opening a bed-and-breakfast," he said.

"That's the hope," she said. "If I can find the right house. It would be nice to work from home, not have to drop the girls off at day care every day. I could make these pretty little breakfasts, maybe even do some homemade jars of jam I could sell to my guests…"

"You surprise me."

"Me?" she said, glancing up at him. "You hardly know me."

"True, but I guess I had a few assumptions going in," he admitted. "You're tougher than I gave you credit for."

"How do you figure that?" she asked with a low laugh.

"Just the way you were handling Ross," he replied. "You seemed to have him under control."

"I did," she said. "I mean, he was on my last nerve, but I was pretty close to sending him away with his tail between his legs."

"You shouldn't have been put in that position to begin with," he replied with a shake of his head. "Tomorrow morning the new cook will start, so we won't have to worry about that anymore."

"That's good. So Peg liked him, then?" she asked.

"She...approved." Colt frowned. "You know, if I didn't know Peg better, I'd say that she sized him up for more than a cook position."

"Oh?"

"I didn't say anything," Colt said. "They're of the same generation, so maybe it was just that."

A rabbit jumped out of the ditch on the side of the road and Jane startled and tripped. Instinctively, Colt shot out his hand and grabbed hers.

Jane's cool fingers wrapped around his hand in a squeeze, and she let out a breathy laugh as they watched the hare bound off into the long grass. She didn't seem to notice that her hand was still in his, and he was about to release her, but somehow he didn't. It felt good. Jane licked her lips and looked up at him. She pulled her hand out of his, and he let go and smiled ruefully.

"Sorry," he murmured.

"It's okay..."

They fell silent then as they walked the rest of the way to the house. Colt's boots thunked against the gravel road, and he inwardly chastised himself. He shouldn't have grabbed her hand like that. What had he been thinking? He hadn't been—it was his own instinct working against him, and he was getting protective of her, it seemed.

He stole a look in her direction, and her cheeks were slightly pink—from the sun or from embarrassment, he wasn't sure. Great. He wasn't much better than Ross right now, was he?

"I didn't mean to do that," he said.

"It's okay," she repeated.

Right. Except it didn't feel okay to him. It felt awkward and strained, and that was the last thing he wanted between them.

"No, I really need you to understand that I'm not making a move on you," he said. "There will be a lot of Rosses in the world who are going to try to get your attention, but I'm not one of those guys."

She sent him a sympathetic look and pulled her hair away from her face in one sweeping motion.

"Not that I don't appreciate…" He grimaced. He wasn't trying to insult her, either. "I work with cattle. A lot. And ranch hands, of course. I manage pasture rotation, sick cows, bullheaded employees. That kind of thing. I'm not the smoothest guy. I'm a straightforward guy who says what he means." He cast about, looking for the right words. "You *are* beautiful, for the record. It's not like I didn't notice."

"It's okay," she said. "I know where you stand."

"Yeah, you know I don't want to get married, but you should know that I'm not the kind of guy who plays around with romance. So if there is ever any question of whether I was flirting or not, maybe just give me the benefit of the doubt." Jane smiled and he eyed her uncertainly. "Okay?"

"Okay. I can do that."

The house was just ahead, and they turned their steps up the hill toward it. The side door was propped open with an old coffee can filled with nails as it normally was when they needed a breeze in there, and Peg looked outside.

"Mommy's coming," Peg said, and the two little girls came scampering out after her.

"Mama!" one of them hollered, and they both came squealing down the short hill toward them.

The toddlers were pretty cute in their matching yellow dresses and their bouncing red curls, and as Jane hoisted up the first toddler, the second girl collided with her knees.

Jane kissed the little girl in her arms, then glanced back at Colt.

"They're getting too big for me to carry together," she said, and her eyes sparkled with a smile. "You want to grab one for me?"

Colt reached for the toddler in her arms, and then she gathered up the other one. The little girl squirmed in his arms and then looked up at him with wide, serious eyes. There was a freckle in the middle of her forehead, and he grinned.

"Hey, Micha," he said quietly.

Micha's face erupted into a smile and she reached for his hat. "Cat!"

He took it off and dropped it onto her head, listening to the sound of her muffled giggles as he matched Jane's pace, walking up toward the house.

Micha pulled his hat off, her hair standing on end, then dropped it back over her face again with a tinkle of laughter.

"She likes my hat," he said, glancing over to find Jane watching him.

"You're good with kids," she said.

"Nah," he replied. "I make a half-decent uncle to my cousins' kids. They call me uncle, at least—it's simpler. I'm the guy who gives cash once a year to cover everything he missed."

Jane laughed and Colt caught Peg's gaze pinned on them, a thoughtful look on her weathered face.

He hadn't had dinner yet, and he smiled in her direction.

"Peg, I'm starving. What do we have?"

"There's a tuna casserole in the fridge," she said. "I thought you would have eaten already at the canteen since Jane was down there."

"I forgot, quite honestly," he said. Tuna casserole meant it was a gift from one of the neighbors. That was a relief. "The casserole will be just fine."

At the steps, he put Micha down so that she could run inside, and Jane passed into the house ahead of him. From the kitchen, he could hear the toddlers babble at their mother. They'd missed her. Well, he wasn't going to be taking her away from them again. He had a cook starting in the morning, and he'd be back to his own workload. Colt stood there in the lowering summer sunlight for a moment, wishing that walk with Jane hadn't felt so nice.

"That's what a family feels like," Peg said quietly, as if reading his thoughts.

He gave her a cautious look. "I'm not a family man, Peg."

"Some families are happy," she said. "It is possible, you know."

It was also possible for a family's sins to shadow the next generation. Colt had never seen a functional and happy marriage up close. He'd certainly seen all the ways to break a heart, though. When he hadn't answered, Peg turned and went into the house, the screen door swinging slowly shut behind her. Peg was right. Some families *were* happy.

"But not ours," he murmured.

Chapter Six

The next morning, Jane woke up at five thirty with the sunrise. The day before had tired her right out, but she wasn't going to be able to sleep any longer. Besides, it felt self-indulgent to sleep in on a ranch that started working at four each morning.

When Jane got up and padded softly to the kitchen, she found Peg at the table with her Bible drinking a cup of coffee in a pool of early morning sunlight that flooded in through an open kitchen window. Some birds twittered outside, and a coffeepot gurgled from the counter, but Peg didn't seem to have heard her, so Jane slipped back to her bedroom and eased the door shut with a soft click. She propped herself up in bed with her own Bible beside her as she listened to her girls breathe. This was a peaceful time of the morning, and she felt a wave of gratefulness for this ranch in spite of it all.

She picked up her Bible and opened it at random, her gaze flowing over the page.

Whither is thy beloved gone, O thou fairest among

women? whither is thy beloved turned aside? that we may seek him with thee.

It was from Song of Solomon, and she sighed and rubbed her hands over her eyes. It seemed that every time she opened her Bible these days, she was opening it to this book. She didn't want to be reminded of marriage, of her early hopes for the lifelong romance she would enjoy. Life hadn't turned out that way. Where had *her* husband gone? First, he'd gone to war, and when he came back his heart still seemed to be out there in the dirt with his brothers at arms. And then he died out there, so far from home. She'd been faithful for as long as he'd lived, but now she was single again. She'd done her duty, and he'd done his. So why, every time she prayed for God's guidance, did she keep coming back to the Song of Solomon with its descriptions of romantic love?

Jane didn't want another marriage! She wanted some quiet, some calm, some time to focus on her children. Wasn't that more important than indulging in some romantic daydream? It hadn't worked out the way she'd hoped the first time, anyway. Life wasn't a poetic romance—it was hard work. But even as she thought it, her mind was moving back to that tall, rugged cowboy, Colt. Their walk together back to the house had felt strangely intimate. He was easy to be with, easy to lean into. That was the problem. If she closed her eyes, she could still feel the sensation of Colt's rough hand closing around hers. His reflexes had been fast, and he'd caught her, stopping her stumble and her heart all at once.

Her eyes fluttered open again. He'd held her hand for a moment—accidentally. He'd made that very clear, and it was a relief, because the last thing she needed was another man who ought to be put in his place. Colt wasn't like that, so she should just stop remembering what that strong hand felt like.

Jane flipped purposefully through her Bible until she got to the verse she was looking for. It was in the seventy-third psalm, and it had been her foundation the last three years.

Whom have I in heaven but thee? and there is none upon earth that I desire beside thee. My flesh and my heart faileth: but God is the strength of my heart, and my portion for ever.

She wasn't alone as long as she had God, and she would continue to count on her Father to provide for her.

Lord, I'm just tired. I know that. Help me not to get my emotions in a tangle right now. I just need some peace...

Jane bent down and brushed Suzie's hair away from her damp forehead. Her daughters deserved a better life than she could provide on her own, and she was grateful that God had prompted her late father-in-law to remember his granddaughters in his will. She didn't need to find another husband to help provide for them. With that inheritance, Jane could do it on her own with pride. God had been listening to her prayers.

When Jane heard the sound of clanking pans from the kitchen, she knew that it was safe to get up and she put her Bible aside.

That morning, Jane helped Peg to clear out a shelf of old books from what had been a personal office. The room was cramped, and besides the bookshelves there were a few boxes, a desk with a clutter of paper and envelopes covering the surface and a filing cabinet in one corner. Most of the books they piled into cartons were paperbacks, a few were fishing manuals and a couple were old cookbooks that Peg said had belonged to Beau's late wife. They boxed them up and carried them out to the black pickup truck that sat outside the house, piling box after box into the bed. The toddlers trailed after them, and as Jane loaded the last box—small, but heavy—Micha and Suzie squatted on the grass, poking at something with a twig.

"Our local library might want these," Peg said. "They have a used book sale every year to raise money, so they could use them for that, too."

"A life boiled down to library book sales and Goodwill runs," Jane said. "Sobering, isn't it?"

"My brother didn't try real hard to endear himself to anyone," Peg replied. "He was lonely, but it was his own fault. He was opinionated and figured anyone who disagreed with him was an idiot. That doesn't make friends."

"Was he always like that?" Jane asked.

"No…" Peg brushed some dust off the front of her shirt. "When we were young, he was different. He got more bitter with age. He was pretty miserable in his marriage, and when Sandra passed away, he only got more miserable."

"Did everyone know it?" Jane asked. "How unhappy they were, I mean."

"It was obvious," Peg replied. "He'd never been terribly in love, at least not that I could tell. But he'd thought she'd be a good ranching wife—and she was! So to hold a grudge against her later for not stirring his heart to poetic heights seems petty to me. He could have been happy with her, if he'd just chosen to be. I was shocked she stayed with him. To live her whole married life unappreciated by her husband—seems like a waste of years, doesn't it?"

Jane was forced to agree with that. "But she stayed..."

"She stayed. She didn't believe in divorce."

Micha and Suzie strayed a little further into the yard and Jane stood there watching them, feeling suddenly sad for these people she'd never met. Josh hadn't talked much about his parents' marriage. Maybe he'd just assumed it was normal. It might explain how distanced he'd been from her when he'd been struggling with his memories from war. She'd tried so hard to be the one he could open up to...

"Was Josh affected by their unhappiness?" she asked after a moment.

"You'd know better than me," Peg replied.

He'd loved her—she knew that—but when he was upset about something, he'd pick fights. Life with Josh hadn't been easy, and maybe his parents' tumultuous marriage explained some of that.

"Well...they're all with God now," Jane said, swallowing a lump in her throat. Whatever problems they'd had in life were over.

Lunch that afternoon consisted of self-made sandwiches and a can of soup. The toddlers were perfectly happy with peanut butter and jam, and after cleaning up, it was time for their nap.

"Maybe I'll just keep sorting through the office while the girls sleep," Jane said.

"You sure you want to?" Peg asked. "You've earned a break, I'd say."

"I'd rather keep my hands busy," she admitted.

So the toddlers drifted off to sleep in the bedroom,

Peg went outside to read in the shade and Jane stood in the center of that office with a cardboard box in one hand and her heart feeling heavy for the father-in-law she'd never properly met.

Beau Marshall had made his share of mistakes, it seemed, and the family he'd left behind had never properly forgiven him for them. Maybe he'd never wanted forgiveness, and they'd sensed that. Jane put the box down on the office chair and picked up some papers from the desktop. Some looked like old bills, others were doodles and notes he'd taken that meant nothing to her. Who knew if these papers would be necessary later for his taxes or something? So Jane gathered them up into a neat pile and started filling the box.

After a few minutes the desktop was clear, and she opened the side drawer. There were pens, paper clips, scraps of paper, broken elastic bands… Most of it was garbage, but deep in the back of the drawer, she pulled out a yellowed envelope.

Inside were a few old snapshots. They were all of Beau and Sandra, by the looks of them. The photos started out with them as a couple in their early forties, both looking serious and some distance between them, but as she worked her way through the pile, the couple got younger and the distance between them shrank; sometimes they were even touching each other in some way. The last photo was their wedding picture, and she was amazed by how much her own husband had looked like his father. Beau and Josh could have been twins in Beau's younger years—the chiseled jaw, the bright red hair, the ice-blue eyes…

And in that wedding picture, Sandra had looked blissful. Just as blissful as Jane had looked on her own wedding day marrying their son. She flipped through the other photos again, looking at those aging faces, and her heart hammered in her throat.

"Would that have been me?" she whispered to herself. If Josh had lived, and if she'd stuck with him because she didn't believe in divorce any more than his mother had...would she have been the sad woman next to a bitter man? Would this have been their future?

Jane sighed, and as she tucked the pictures away she saw a handwritten note. She pulled it out, but before she even saw the signature she knew it was Josh's writing:

Happy Anniversary, Mom and Dad.

Only that. So their son had collected those pictures. Maybe he'd hoped to do something more with them, and to Beau's credit, he had kept them in his desk. Or shoved them there. For whatever reason, a couple that had started out happily enough had turned chilly and distant.

What would a marriage like Beau and Sandra's do to the children? If Josh and Jane had ended up the same way, what would it have done to the girls? It was an awful thought, and she shivered in spite of the warmth.

Maybe it was better not to dwell on what-ifs.

Jane opened the next drawer. This one was more cluttered, and she pulled out a tattered old map, a half-full box of tissues, a few different pads of writing paper, a box of staples... And underneath it all, a handle of some sort glimmered in the light. She reached down and grabbed it, pulling up a pearl-handled handgun. She looked down at it in shock. It was awfully tarnished. If Beau had antiques, why didn't he take better care of them?

A sound behind her startled her, she spun around, the

gun still in her hand and she saw Colt in the doorway, a surprised look on his face. He raised his hands slowly.

"You want to put that thing down?" he asked, his tone low but cautious.

"Sorry." She put it onto the desk with a short laugh. "Do you think it's loaded?"

"No idea. I just don't like guns pointed at me," he said.

"It's your uncle's?" she asked.

"Yeah, he had a few around the house." Colt came into the office and picked up the gun, turning it over in his hand. He opened it, shook out a bullet and held it up.

"Oh!" she gasped. "It *was* loaded!"

"Beau always said that when he needed a gun, he needed a bullet, too," Colt said, and he put the gun down again. "Sorry about that. I thought I'd found all his handguns. If I thought there was a gun rattling around here with kids in the house—"

"It's okay," she said. "You sure there aren't any more?"

"I've checked everywhere," he said. "Still, we should stay vigilant with the girls."

She nodded. "I always do."

Colt met her gaze and he held it for a moment. "You want some help in here?"

"I wouldn't turn it down." She tossed the old, folded map into the box. "I thought you said you'd be busy."

"I am." He gave her a rueful smile, then picked up a box from the corner and looked inside. "But I'm the boss now."

She wasn't going to complain. It would be nice to have some company as she rooted through the remnants of a stranger's life. She'd thought she wanted some time to herself, but now that he was here she realized she was glad.

Colt hadn't exactly planned to come sort through the office with Jane, but he'd been thinking about her all morning and when he found himself with a couple of hours to spare…well, he found himself headed back to the house. He'd told himself he should lend a hand in clearing things out, but it was more than that. He missed her.

Colt glanced over at Jane, and she looked tense. Her gaze was clouded and she tossed items from the drawer into a box with more force than was necessary.

"You okay?" he asked after a moment.

She shut the drawer and looked up at him. "Beau and Josh—they looked almost identical when Beau was young."

"Yeah." He wasn't sure what she was getting at.

"These pictures—" She pulled out an envelope and handed them over. "The wedding photo. That could be Josh!"

"He looked like his dad." Colt squinted at her. "It happens in families."

"I know…" She sighed. "It's nothing. I'm just—"

She didn't finish, but she seemed to visibly rally herself and she smiled quickly at him. She was covering up whatever had rattled her, and he wished she wouldn't.

"What was bugging you?" he asked. He flipped through the photos of his aunt and uncle, then looked over at her quizzically. "Josh put these together for his parents one year for their anniversary. I think it was the year before his mom died."

"That might explain why Beau kept them close," she said quietly and when Colt continued to look at her she added, "He wasn't a great husband, from what I've heard, but he must have loved her in his own way, I guess."

So she was seeing the family problem, was she? Colt sucked in a breath. "Neither of us got a great example of how a functional marriage worked."

"I was talking with Peg earlier," she observed. "And she said she didn't know why Sandra stuck it out. And I look at those photos, and I wonder if I wouldn't have been in Sandra's shoes in twenty years."

"They were a...unique couple," Colt said carefully.

"They started out happy—" She reached for the pictures and pulled out the wedding photo. "Josh and I had one almost identical to this one. This could be Josh—the exact same expression."

Colt looked down at the photo, and he could see what Jane was talking about. They'd started out looking pretty happy. Wasn't that the fear, though? That whatever seemed to dog the Marshall marriages would cling to the next generation?

"I've been hearing about Sandra from Peg," Jane said. "She stuck it out. She wouldn't leave him, and it sounds like he wasn't very good to her."

Colt nodded. "True."

"But sticking around—that didn't help, did it? Peg suggested that maybe they got married for the wrong reasons. Maybe Beau didn't love her enough, or something like that. But how was Sandra supposed to know that?"

This had really upset her, and Colt wasn't sure what

to say. This had been the problem all along for him—seeing marriages go sour before his eyes.

"I know," he said at last. "I don't know what to say. But you're right."

"That could have been *me*," she said, then she licked her lips and looked away.

Jane—unloved and resentful. It seemed impossible looking at how beautiful and vulnerable she was standing there. Could any red-blooded male turn off his heart with her? But relationships weren't so simple, and Sandra had been young and beautiful once, too. The men in this family seemed to have a track record of messing things up with women who didn't deserve them.

"I guess that's what we're all a little scared of," he said after a beat or two of silence.

"The more I hear about Beau, the more he sounds like Josh," she said quietly. "Josh was hard to be close to. He pulled back, didn't share easily. And hearing about his parents' marriage, I guess it makes sense that he'd have a few trust issues. But I'm sure Beau had his own reasons for becoming the bitter man he was, too."

"Hey, Josh loved you enough to keep you away from this place," Colt said, stepping closer to her and catching her hand with his. "And maybe he didn't know how to have a functional relationship, but the fact that he kept you away from here says that he was at least trying to keep all of this from affecting what he had with you."

"And I'm here because I want that family for my girls…" Jane looked up at him, and she didn't pull her hand back. Sadness swam in her eyes. "I was hoping to find some family connection, not some foreshadowing of a miserable future together had he lived…"

"You wanted some memories," he said. "Some insights into why he hated strawberry ice cream. Some stories to tell your daughters."

"Why did he hate strawberry ice cream?" she asked.

Colt smiled sorrowfully. "He ate it one year when he got the flu and threw it up. Never could eat it again."

"Oh…" She smiled sadly. "Yeah, that was the kind of thing I wanted to know. What else?"

"I don't know…" He cast about in his memories for something she might like. "We built a tree house together as kids. It was a good one—like really solid and respectable. We used to hang out in it all the way into our teens. We could talk there, open up."

"What did you talk about?" she asked.

"Our hopes for the future," he said with a shrug. "Josh would talk it out when he was mad at his dad. Which was often. I went there and cried when my mom left. She'd told me it was better for my future if I stayed and kept working with Beau. I'd wanted her to tell me to come with her, leave it all behind… And she'd told me it was a smarter choice to stay. I was only sixteen. I felt so grown-up right up until my mom drove away, and then I felt like a kid and cried my heart out in that tree house. It was Josh who eventually came out to find me."

"Why didn't you go with her?" Jane asked.

"Because Beau had already mentioned leaving me a part of the ranch," Colt admitted, his throat tight. "You have no idea how much I sacrificed for this place."

They were silent for a few beats, then Jane heaved a sigh.

"Josh talked about that tree house," she said. "He'd been proud of the workmanship. It meant a lot to him, too, but there was so much he left out when he told me stories… He held back a lot. Even from me."

"I'm sorry," Colt said, and he moved his fingers over hers, wishing he could pull her into his arms and just hold her for a little while. It would be comforting for him, too, right now. But Jane didn't deserve this heartache either, and looking down into those dark eyes, he wished he had something to say to make it better.

She was so close that he could make out the scent of her perfume, and he could see the soft flutter of her pulse at the base of her neck. A strand of hair fell across her forehead. Without thinking, he lifted his free hand to brush it aside, but as his fingers touched her skin, his gaze flickered down to those pink lips. She opened her mouth as if about to say something but she didn't; he found himself transfixed by her mouth, and a deep instinct inside him was tugging him closer.

She was both beautiful and sad, and he longed to comfort her somehow. He wanted to tug her into his arms and hold her close… But his gaze kept dropping down to her lips, and it was like the rest of the room had evaporated around them, leaving just the two of them, the soft flutter of her pulse and this yearning to cover those lips with his own.

A clatter from the kitchen made them both start, and Colt dropped her hand and took a step back. He cleared his throat.

"Sorry," she said quickly. "My problems with Josh are still private—"

"Hey, it's okay," he said. "You have to talk to someone. And I'm okay if that's me. I can handle it. Of anyone, I understand where Josh came from."

"But now he's gone," she said, her voice shaking. "It isn't right to tell our secrets now. He deserves to be remembered better than that."

"And he is," Colt said quietly. "I promise you that."

Colt had had a whole childhood with Josh, an adolescence. They'd shared everything growing up, built a tree house together, and in that tree house he'd heard about the girls Josh had crushes on, he'd known about Josh's hopes to join the army before anyone else had. Josh and Colt had come from the same fractured family, and Colt understood.

"We were happy," Jane said firmly. Trying to convince him? He wasn't sure. But if a woman was so tired after a marriage that she didn't want love again, then he was willing to guess that she wasn't as happy as she declared.

"Pretending things were better than they were isn't going to comfort him. He's past our fumbling attempts to fix it, isn't he? I know you loved him with all you had, Jane. And that's all you could give. You did your best."

"It wasn't enough," she said, and tears misted her eyes.

Love never seemed to be quite enough to keep two well-meaning people together…or at least to keep them happy, and that knowledge had settled into his own heart years ago.

"We're kind of a mess here," he said, his voice tight with repressed emotion. "I was honest about that from the start."

Jane shrugged. "Apparently, so am I."

If nothing else, she was in good company.

"I'd better get back to work," he said quickly.

"Yeah, of course."

He met her gaze one last time, then turned for the door. Colt had idealized his aunt and uncle's relationship because they were married still—unlike his own parents. But the more he saw of their actual relationship, the warier he felt about a marriage of his own one day. So far, he'd experienced a dad who walked away, and an aunt and uncle who made each other miserable. It had made him suspicious of the other married relationships he saw in the family at a greater distance. People hid their worst. Colt wasn't so different from Josh. He'd just realized how messed up he was earlier than his cousin had. But they both came from the same family, had been raised with the same issues, and running away hadn't helped Josh as much as he'd thought.

But Colt didn't want to think about any of that right now. Sometimes it was easier to just push it aside and get back out to the field where his problems seemed smaller under the wide, cloudless sky.

Chapter Seven

Jane stood in the empty office, staring at the doorway. She held a stray piece of paper in her hand, and when she realized it she dropped it into the box.

What had just happened here? She'd opened up much more than she'd intended. She hadn't meant to say so much, it had just been stewing around inside her and with Colt looking down into her eyes like that, she'd found herself wanting to talk. It had been a long time since she'd had someone who cared like that.

Maybe it was that he could understand better than anyone else…but there had been a look in his eye that Jane recognized. She'd been married, after all. She knew what it looked like when a man was thinking about closing the distance between them. He'd been intense and focused, and even remembering it made her legs feel a little weak.

Colt had been thinking of kissing her.

She licked her lips, and her fingers fluttered up to her mouth. Why was she even entertaining this thought? Obviously, she couldn't kiss him. That would be ridiculous, but that moment couldn't be dismissed quite so easily, either. There was obviously some attraction between them. She'd have to be careful. The worst thing she could do right now would be to allow her loneliness to direct her steps. That was God's job.

That evening, Jane tried to help Peg in the kitchen but the older woman kept brushing her off.

"I know what Colt likes," Peg said. "You're a guest here, anyway. Your girls need you. I can do this on autopilot."

So Jane did as Peg asked and left her alone in the kitchen. She got the girls into the bath and cleaned them up. Micha got loose and ran naked around the house shrieking in delight until Jane caught her, dried her off and got her into her pajamas. Suzie was quieter this evening, and while Jane combed their wet hair, they played with their dollies.

The smells of cooking coming from the kitchen weren't exactly appetizing, but Jane wasn't going to complain. She had a few more days here, and then she'd be going back to her life in Minneapolis. She'd find a new job for a little while until she sorted out how exactly she'd open that bed-and-breakfast, but a future was finally opening up in front of her.

Her phone blipped and she picked it up to see a text from a work friend.

Jane, can you cover my Saturday shift? I've got a family thing. Let me know!

Apparently, one of them hadn't heard that she'd been a victim of the last wave of layoffs. She sighed and put the phone back down without response. She hadn't been close enough with any of her work friends to even tell them that she was leaving town. Colt had been right—she did need someone she could talk to, but with her husband's passing she'd lost the camaraderie with the military wives. Widowhood affected all of her relationships.

It was time to start over.

From the bedroom, Jane heard the side door bang shut, and the bass notes of Colt's voice reverberating from the other room. Jane picked up the bedtime storybook that her girls loved and waited for them in the hallway.

"Come on, Micha," she said. "Suzie, come on."

The girls picked up their dolls and followed her down the hall toward the living room. She emerged into the room at the same time Colt came in from the kitchen.

"Hey," he said.

"Hi." She stopped short and smiled hesitantly, and they were both silent for a moment. She glanced over as Micha and Suzie pulled a throw blanket off the couch and entertained themselves by rolling in it and giggling together.

"Look, Colt, I'm sorry about earlier," she said quickly, keeping her tone low. "I shouldn't have vented on you like that. It wasn't fair to you, and it was—"

"You were fine," he interrupted, and he closed the distance between them in two quick strides. He was suddenly so close that her breath caught in her throat and she looked at him, her thoughts draining from her head.

"Jane, I think we can count as friends at this point, can't we?" he asked softly.

Friends didn't come that close to kissing each other, but he had a point, and to their credit they hadn't crossed any lines. And maybe she'd misread the situation.

"I think so," she said.

"Well, friends talk. They open up. You weren't out of line, okay? If anyone was, it was me."

They were adults with self-control and they could keep things solidly on the side of friendship if they wanted to.

"Dinner is going to take another half hour," Peg said, poking her head into the room, and Colt took a step back. She held two plates in her hands, and she glanced between Colt and Jane. "Everything okay?"

"Fine," Colt said brusquely.

"You might as well have some apple crisp," Peg added. "There's some left over. But you promise me you'll eat supper."

Peg deposited the plates onto the coffee table, two grayish masses, one tan slice of apple showing on top of one plate.

"Mmm." Colt seemed to be trying to look enthusiastic, but it didn't make it to his eyes. He glanced over at Jane and she sent him a sympathetic look.

"Hold on," Jane said. "I saw a can of whipped cream in the fridge."

"Yeah?" Colt said, and she had to smile at the hope in his voice.

Jane went into the kitchen, pulled the can of whipped cream out of the fridge and gave it a shake.

"You sure you won't let me give you a hand?" Jane asked Peg.

"It's just a matter of waiting on it," Peg said, glancing up from where she was working on a crossword. She looked over at the oven, then back down at the crossword. "Half an hour," she repeated. "Give or take."

Jane headed back into the living room where Colt was now seated on the couch and the girls were covering his knees with the throw blanket.

"Nigh-nigh…" Suzie said, patting Colt's knee under the blanket. "Nigh-nigh…"

"Kiss," said Micha, and she kissed his knee with tiny pursed lips. "Nigh-nigh…"

"They're tucking you in," Jane said with a laugh.

"Yeah, it looks that way," he said. "Are you putting me to bed already?"

"Nigh-nigh, Cat," Micha said seriously holding up one finger in an imitation of Jane, and Jane rolled her eyes then held up the whipped cream.

"Want some?" Jane asked.

"Yeah, that would be great," he said, holding out his plate.

"No!" Micha said reproachfully. "Nigh-nigh!"

Jane sprayed a fluffy coil of whipped cream onto his crisp, and then did the same for her own.

"Come have a bite," Jane said to her daughters, sinking into the couch next to Colt, and the girls were placated with mouthfuls of crisp.

"The whipped cream helps." Colt smiled, then turned his attention to his plate.

Jane smiled back and took another bite. It did help— a simple sweet treat could cover over a whole multitude of awkward mistakes. She was going to have to start fresh in every other aspect of her life, so maybe she could start over with Colt, too.

He was family. If her girls were going to have a relationship with their dad's side of the family, then she needed him.

Colt watched as Jane fed Micha a bite of her crisp, Jane opening her mouth in an unconscious mimic of her child. Mother and daughter smiled into each other's eyes.

"Yummy?" Jane said. "It's good, right?" Then she turned to Suzie, her fork held aloft. "Open... Mmmm. Yummy, right?"

It was such an ordinary moment, but Jane glowed in a special way when she was talking to her little girls. It was like they lit up a place inside her that no one else could touch, and he had a hard time tearing his gaze away. She tucked her veil of dark hair behind her ear, a small golden earring sparkling in the sunlight that flooded in from the living room window. He hadn't noticed those earrings before...

He tore his gaze away from it. He had to keep his feet on the ground here.

"Tomorrow is Sunday," Colt said quietly.

"That's right. It is." Jane looked over at him.

"Are you a churchgoer?"

"I normally am," Jane said. "When I can get there. Everything's more complicated with twins."

"Yeah, I could see that." He cleared his throat. "I go every week, myself. So... I'd be going tomorrow. If you want to come along, I'd be happy to drive you. It's just a little church on a side road—not so easy to find if you don't know where you're going."

"Yes, that would be nice." She smiled. "Thanks, Colt."

He felt gratified to know he could do something for her—make this a bit easier.

"Sure. No problem."

Colt realized he was looking forward to this, probably more than he should. The thing was, he cared for Jane. She was a good woman, and she deserved better than any of them could offer. A good woman couldn't fix a broken family.

"Supper." Peg's tart voice snapped his attention away from Jane, and he rose to his feet.

"Right. Thanks, Peg," he said, but when his aunt looked at him, she raised an eyebrow just a little and he felt some heat hit his face. No doubt she was jumping to all sorts of conclusions right now.

But Colt wasn't trying to start something with Jane. If anything, he was trying to protect her. He could say that he was doing it for Josh, but he wasn't. He was doing this for himself—and if he could do well by Jane, when she went back to her life, here was hoping he wouldn't be filled with regrets.

Supper consisted of some dry meatloaf that was salvageable with ketchup on top. The potatoes were quite good, though, and the boiled veggies were downright passable with some butter melting on top of them. Overall, it wasn't too bad and Colt was too hungry to chew too much anyway.

When Jane took the toddlers to brush their teeth, Colt stayed at the table, his elbows planted in front of him. Peg rose to her feet and started gathering plates.

"Leave that," Colt said. "I'll take care of it."

"I won't complain about that," Peg said and she smiled. She paused with her hands on the back of her chair. "She's nice, isn't she?"

"Jane?" he asked, as if there were anyone else for Peg to be commenting on.

Peg smiled but didn't look fooled. "I don't like just anyone, but she's...decent. A good mother, too."

"Yeah, well..." Colt wasn't sure what he could say to that, so he picked up the plates and brought them to the counter. He turned back to see his aunt heading out of the kitchen. "Peg?"

She turned around. "Hmm?"

"Why did Beau leave me the ranch?" he asked.

"You know why," she said with a shake of her head. "You wanted to actually ranch this land. Josh didn't."

"I wanted this," Colt admitted quietly. "I *really* wanted it."

"And that makes you feel guilty," Peg concluded.

He looked over at the older woman, then shrugged helplessly. "I was the nephew. I shouldn't have been put in the will ahead of Josh. We all knew that. Beau was wrong."

"Beau was wrong about a lot of things," Peg replied. "You know how he was. He was so determined that Josh do things his way that he couldn't see past his own ideas. He'd always been like that. You were more like him."

"I'm not sure that's a compliment," Colt said bitterly.

"You know what I mean," Peg said, softening her tone. "You loved the land. You wanted to raise cattle. You wanted to keep this ranch in the family, and that meant a lot to Beau. He wished Josh could have been more like you."

"It tore Josh and me apart," Colt said. "That stupid will…"

"That stupid will has put you in a very good position," Peg countered. "You wanted to ranch, and now you own your own land. That's something some men can only dream of. Be grateful that he gave it to you, and not someone else. Because Josh wasn't getting this land."

"When Josh found out about the will, he came and asked me to talk to his dad with him," Colt confessed.

"He asked me to tell Beau that I didn't want to own the land. That I liked things as they were."

"But you didn't like it," Peg replied. "You were working long hours, you were getting paid a fair wage, but it wasn't much. And you wanted more for your life than to be working for your uncle, and later your cousin."

"I could have gone elsewhere," he conceded.

"Listen, Colt. You had someone offer you a ranch of your own, and you jumped at it," Peg said. "I can't say that I blame you. No one does."

"If I hadn't jumped at it, Josh might have stuck around," he countered.

"You couldn't have known," Peg replied.

"That doesn't make it any less my fault," he replied quietly. "Beau offered me what I wanted most, and I sacrificed my relationship with my cousin to get it."

"Even if you'd told him you didn't want it, Beau might have still left the ranch to you," Peg said quietly. "He loved you, Colt. You were a cowboy at heart, and he understood how you ticked. You loved the dirt under your boots in the same way that he did. You cared about the ranch, the cattle, the legacy of this place. That was more than he could say about Josh. He loved his son, too, but he didn't understand him. Josh was cut from different cloth than you and Beau were. Was that a tragedy? Of course. But you can't blame yourself for all the ways Beau failed as a father. Your uncle loved you. I'm sorry that his love came at such a high price."

Colt stuck the plug in the sink and turned on the water. "Thanks, Peg. You're probably right."

Peg stood still by the doorway, watching him as he squirted dish soap into the water and piled dishes on the counter next to him. He glanced back at her. Worry creased her lined face, and she tapped one hand against her arm testily.

"We all just do our best, Colt," she said after a moment. "Age doesn't give any great wisdom. You young people expect us to have the answers, but we don't. Sometimes we mess up royally, like Beau did. But I knew he meant well."

"It's not enough, though, is it?" he said. "Josh is still dead."

Peg sighed. "One day you'll be old, too, Colt. And you'll understand then. It won't matter what the younger generations expect from you, you'll only be able to be yourself. With all your limitations intact."

"You think I should forgive Beau," he said.

"Yes," she said simply. "And while you're at it, I think you should forgive yourself."

Peg turned and left the room, and Colt stood motionless for a moment, her words sinking in. Maybe she was right. Wasn't this what he'd been saying all along—that he couldn't change who he was or the family he'd come from? Even age didn't seem to improve what this family could offer.

Beau had messed things up, but that could just as easily be Colt. Listening to Jane talk, Josh was just as screwed up as the rest of them. So why did this bother him afresh? He'd already decided not to inflict himself on a wife and kids.

But it did bug him. Because now when he allowed himself a tiny glimpse of a future with a family, he found Jane's face in his mind. And that was ridiculous. She'd already been let down by one man in this family, and Colt couldn't claim to be any better.

Lord, keep me grounded, he silently prayed.

Colt's cell phone rang, and he dried his hands then picked it up.

"Yeah," he said.

"Colt? This is Bruce Armson, up the road."

"Bruce," Colt said. "How are you?"

"Not bad. How are you holding up?" Bruce asked.

"I'm okay. I've inherited the ranch, if you hadn't heard."

"I did, actually," Bruce admitted. "Word travels fast. Your uncle made the right choice, in my opinion. I was calling because I have a proposition for you."

"Oh yeah?"

"There's a strip of land that butts up against mine, and I've wanted to own it for some time now. Beau never did want to sell, but I was wondering if you might be of a different mind than he was?"

"Wait…" Colt mentally swept over the land in his mind. There was a strip of land between Bruce's fields and a stream, and Colt was familiar with it. He'd spent a good amount of his boyhood on that land building a tree house with Josh. "I know the land you're talking about, but I'm not sure I'm interested in selling it."

"I'm not looking to rip you off here," Bruce said, and then named a price. Colt's breath caught in his throat.

"Say that again?"

Bruce obliged. "What do you say?"

It was enough money to pay Jane for the cattle. He wouldn't have to accrue any more debt than he already carried, and that would be a real blessing right about now. It would solve his main problem, which was buying his cattle back from Jane. But he couldn't quite agree to it—not yet.

"I'll have to think it over, Bruce," he said. "But I'm thinking real seriously about it. Trust me."

"Glad to hear that. Call me when you've made up your mind either way."

"Will do. Take care now."

Colt hung up the phone and put it down on the counter next to him. He hadn't been back to the tree house in more than a decade, and he wasn't even sure what was left of it. But selling it—it felt like another betrayal.

From deep in the house, he could hear a woman's voice softly singing. He couldn't make out the words, but he recognized a lullaby and he stopped short, listening. That would be Jane singing to her daughters, and the tune was so wistful and haunting that it seemed to wrap around his chest like a vise.

Once upon a time, everything had been relatively simple. It had been him and Mom, and they'd taken care of each other. All he'd wanted was to make a little extra money so his mom wouldn't have to worry about the bills so much. Just his daily bread—that's what he'd prayed for.

When he'd built that tree house with his cousin, they used to talk about the future they'd have when they were both man enough to make a difference. Colt's dreams had all surrounded providing for his mother. He'd buy her a house one day. He'd get her a shiny pickup truck that wouldn't break down. He'd pay all her bills so that she wouldn't have to worry anymore. When he was grown up, his family would be different. His kids would be happy. He'd be nice to his wife…

Now that Colt had this ranch, it wasn't quite so simple anymore. He was in debt, his options were limited, and every choice he made seemed to bring him closer and closer to becoming just like his uncle. Sometimes a man didn't choose a destructive path—sometimes he stumbled onto it without even realizing it. His boyhood longing to fix it all was just a naive fantasy. Now that he'd finally grown up, he'd simply joined the mess.

Chapter Eight

Jane dug through the suitcase and came up with two lit-tle matching church dresses. They'd been a baby shower gift, and when she'd seen the toddler sizes next to her tiny newborns, she'd thought they would never fit. Now she was grateful for the older woman's foresight in in-cluding a few larger sizes in the pile of clothes she'd given Jane.

"Whoops! Where are you going?"

Jane jogged after Suzie, who'd made a diaper-clad escape down the hallway, and carried her back into the bedroom. She shut the door tightly behind her and put the toddler down next to her sister.

"Time to get dressed for church," Jane said. "Come here, Suzie. You first."

The dresses were almost too small on the girls. They seemed to be growing so fast that they could be into a dress and out of it again before they even managed to stain it. But looking down at the dresses that were a little snug around the chest already made her heart beat just a bit faster. She'd known that raising two kids at once would be expensive, but they cost even more than she'd imagined and the constant pressure to keep providing all the necessities was taxing.

When the money came from the inheritance, would she dare use it for things like church dresses? Or would she be too cautious to touch it for anything less than the bed-and-breakfast? She didn't know yet. She was still praying about that—she needed guidance. One thing was for sure, her own wardrobe could wait. The pink dress that she'd worn to the lawyer's office was the best that she owned, and she wore it every week to church during the warm months.

When Jane had finished dressing the girls, she opened the door and they both exploded into the hallway in a torrent of giggles and pattering feet. Jane could hear the shower going, and she could only assume that Peg was getting ready for church as well.

The girls flung themselves onto the couch, where they climbed around and babbled to each other. Jane smiled at their antics and headed into the kitchen. All she wanted right now was a strong cup of coffee.

The side door opened and Colt came inside just as she entered the kitchen. He tossed his hat onto a peg and sat down to pull off his boots.

"Morning," he said.

"Good morning. I'm getting myself some coffee. Do you want some, too?"

"Yeah, that would be great. Just black," Colt said. "One of my ranch hands is hungover, so I had to pitch in with chores this morning."

"Hungover?" Jane said. "I'm sure that went over well."

"Yeah." He chuckled. "I'd fire him if I had any wiggle room right now. As it is, I gave him a stiff warning,

I'm docking him a day of pay and here's hoping that will be deterrent enough."

"Sure hope so." She poured two mugs of coffee and slid one toward him, then put some sugar into her own.

"So, I got a call last night from a neighbor who wants to buy a stretch of land that butts up against his," Colt said.

Jane looked up. "Oh?"

"I could pay you out pretty easily if I sold to him. That's the good news," Colt said, but there was a hesitant look in his eye. He took a sip of coffee, then put the mug down on the counter with a thunk.

"And the problem?" she asked.

"It's the land where we built that tree house."

Jane's heart skipped a beat. She knew what that patch of land meant to Colt—he couldn't sell it for her. She shook her head. "So you said no, right?"

"I said I'd think about it real seriously," he replied.

"But you love that place," she countered. "The memories—"

"Sometimes a guy has to be practical," Colt replied.

And it wasn't hers. She had no say. Jane heaved a sigh. "Josh said it had two levels and a rope swing."

"Yeah, it was pretty impressive." He pursed his lips. "Or it seemed so back then. I'm sure if I see it again I'll be less impressed with our feats of engineering."

"It's not about that, though," she said.

"Back when we used to go out to the tree house and talk, our problems seemed fixable. We honestly thought there were solutions. Maybe I miss that youthful optimism."

Jane looked into the living room where her girls were still tumbling on the couch together. She was doing her best with them, but would they have similar childhood memories, longing to fix the stuff that she messed up?

"It meant more to you than it did to Josh, didn't it?" she asked.

"I think so," he admitted. "It's different being the one left behind. My mom drove away. He might have fought with his dad, but his dad was still here. I guess I counted on Josh more than I realized back then. I probably counted on stuff like that tree house, because it was nailed down, and it wasn't going anywhere. Not that I went out there much when I was older, but knowing it was still there helped in some weird way."

"*Will* you sell it?" she asked.

"I don't know." He sighed. "I want to ride out and take a look at it again. I probably can't really get around selling it, but I can at least see it one last time."

"Maybe your neighbor will let you visit the treehouse from time to time."

"Whether he does or not, before I sell, I need to go take a look at it. I'll know what's right once I see it again."

"I'd love to see it, too," she admitted, then she stopped herself. She couldn't just invite herself along on Colt's personal goodbye to a cherished spot. "Sorry. I'm not trying to intrude. I know that this one is personal for you—"

"Hey, it was important to Josh, too. So I can understand you wanting to come along." Colt met her gaze. "I'm thinking of riding out tomorrow morning. It would only take about an hour. Do you ride?"

"Fairly well," she said. "I'd go with you if we could bring the girls."

He sobered at that, then fell silent. She was overstepping—she could feel it. She was used to adapting every part of her life to her girls, but that didn't mean everyone else wanted to do the same.

"That's too much to ask," she said quickly. "Never mind. You go and do what you need to. There are some things that belonged between you and Josh."

Colt was silent for a moment, then he asked, "Have they been on horseback before? A friend of mine used to take his son on trail rides when he was about two. He just put him in front of him on the saddle. I mean, do you think it would work?"

"You don't have to bring us out there," she said. "I'm serious."

"Hey, if I'm going to sell it, you should see it once," he countered. "You're the only one who'd understand it…you know?"

And she did. It was his last connection to his cousin, and maybe even more than that. She'd clung to a few connections of her own, like her wedding rings that sat in a little mother-of-pearl box in the bottom of her suitcase.

"I'm sorry you have to sell because of me."

"I don't blame you," he said, and she smiled ever so slightly. "I blame Beau."

She wasn't sure if he was joking or not, and she eyed him for a moment.

"Hey, I'm glad that you were left something," he went on. "Josh would have wanted that, and obviously Beau did, too. It complicates things for me, but it's not the end of the world."

"But that land—" she started.

"New beginnings," he said, cutting her off. "Things are going to change around here. There's no getting around that. I'm not Beau, and those days are gone. Besides, sometimes the stuff we remember wasn't quite so pristine as we thought."

Fair enough. Nothing had been as pristine as Jane had hoped, either. Not marriage, not motherhood… Life was harder than anyone anticipated, and maybe it was for the best not to see it coming.

"Let's ride out tomorrow," he said. "I'll borrow some toddler helmets, and we can pack a lunch."

"You sure?" she asked.

"I wouldn't turn down the company," he said, his voice a low rumble. His dark gaze met hers, and she felt that intensity again—and her breath caught in her throat.

"Mama, cracker!" a little voice said, and Jane looked over to see her girls come into the kitchen, eyes bright and hair already tangled from play.

"I'd better go take a shower," Colt said. "We leave for church in half an hour."

As Colt headed toward the stairs that led down to his place, Jane watched him go. This inheritance was tearing apart some precious memories for this man, and she couldn't help but feel bad for that. But maybe a ride out there would be healing in some small way.

For both of them. In very different ways, they both needed to lay Joshua Marshall to rest.

Colt's mind was on that land as they drove along the gravel roads, small rocks whipping up and rattling against the side of the truck as he went. It was a fair offer, and it would help him out of a bind, but letting go of that land was going to mean lifting the lid on stuff he didn't want to look at. He'd just buried his uncle—couldn't that be enough for a while?

But Jane was here, the offer was on the table and he had to pay her somehow for those cattle. More debt wouldn't be wise since he'd inherited this place with a pile of debt attached to it. But this was Sunday, and he normally tried not to think about the business pressures for one day a week. If possible.

Lord, what do I do? he silently prayed. *I need You to show me the way.*

The church was coming up on the left, and Colt slowed and signaled his turn. Venton Country Church was located along a back road, nestled between a stretch of trees and pasture. The town of Creekside had a church, too, but the cowboys tended to come out this way because the worship style was more bluegrass and country. They didn't even have a regular pastor at the moment. A retired minister was volunteering his time for two weeks a month, and other than that they filled the service with some testimonies and rousing gospel music.

They were a little late. The parking lot was already full of pickup trucks and he could hear the familiar cords of some banjo music filtering out of the old church.

"This is it," Colt said, then he glanced into the backseat where the toddlers were eating Cheerios out of little plastic tubs. "They have a Sunday school here during the sermon, I think. I've never done the kid thing before, so—"

"They're a little young for Sunday school," Jane said with a smile. "I just take them with me into the service and sit in the back, if that works for you."

"Sure. Yeah." That seemed simple enough. "Let's do it."

Getting the girls out of their car seats was simpler than he anticipated. Jane grabbed a cloth bag, tossed it over her shoulder and then lifted Micha down to the ground.

"Stay here," Jane said firmly, then climbed into the truck to fetch Suzie.

Colt and Micha exchanged a solemn look. It seemed that Micha knew that tone in her mother's voice and didn't appear inclined to disobey. Jane emerged from the truck, Suzie in her arms.

"Ready," she said, and Colt slammed shut the truck door.

When he'd asked her to come with him to church, it had been impulsive, just wanting a little more time with her. But now that he was looking at the toddlers, the bag over Jane's shoulder and impish look in Micha's eye, he had a fleeting feeling of misgiving. He was very likely in over his head.

Colt carried Micha in his arms, and Jane had Suzie. They made their way up the wooden steps, and he pulled open the front door, letting her go inside first. The music echoed through the foyer, and when he pushed open the swinging door to the sanctuary, there was an empty pew in the back. They slipped into the space and Jane dropped her bag to the seat beside them. Everyone was standing, singing along with a familiar song, so no one noticed their arrival.

When the song service was over, everyone sat down and Jane's warm arm brushed against his. It felt comforting, close. It was only one week—it's not like he was going to get used to this. Suzie squirmed on her mother's lap, reaching forward for a hymnal just as Micha tossed a handful of Cheerios to the ground. He'd seen parents giving their kids snacks in church before, and now he thought he understood why. It might be a bit messy, but at least it kept those little hands busy. Jane leaned forward to pick the Cheerios up, her arm moving against Colt's leg as she stretched to reach them. Jane straightened again, put the Cheerios into a tissue and wrapped them up.

"Enough, Micha," Jane whispered. "No throwing. Be good."

Micha started to squirm in Colt's lap, so he scooted over and put her down on the seat between himself and Jane. Jane smiled, and then scooted further over, putting Suzie down on the bench next to her sister. Jane felt far away, and Colt slid his arm along the back of the pew just to be more comfortable. His finger came to rest against her shoulder and he froze. Was that too much?

Jane didn't seem to notice his touch, so he didn't move. She handed out more Cheerios to the girls and when Micha looked ready to throw one, Jane raised a finger and eyed her meaningfully. The little girl popped the Cheerio in her mouth instead and smiled sweetly.

Colt couldn't help but chuckle silently. This kid— she was a handful!

The sermon that Sunday was about the prodigal son—strangely appropriate. Except the Marshall prodigal son never had returned. If he hadn't died, would he have come back eventually? Maybe Josh would have made it home before Beau died. Because knowing Jane like he did now, she seemed like the kind of woman Josh would have needed—strong, soft, convinced about what was right.

But Josh hadn't lived, and she'd returned in his place.

Colt smelled something, and he looked over at Jane with a half smile. She grimaced, leaned down to sniff between the two girls and picked up Suzie.

"I have to change her," Jane whispered. "Can you just watch Micha for me? I won't be long."

"Yeah, sure." He said it before he'd even thought about it, and by the time he thought twice, Jane was already standing up and grabbing the cloth bag. She slipped past his knees, her pink dress catching on his jeans as she slid by. Micha looked after her mother, and her lip started to quiver.

"It's okay," Colt whispered. "Mommy's coming back in a minute."

Micha leaned forward, watching as Jane disappeared out the swinging doors that led into the church foyer, then she sighed and picked up her cup of Cheerios again. Maybe this wouldn't be so bad, after all. He glanced instinctively toward the door where Jane had disappeared.

"Mommy," Micha said, her voice rising. "Mommy?"

"Hey, it's okay," Colt whispered and he scooped her up and sat her onto his knee. "She's coming right back, Micha. Okay? Watch that door. She'll come right back."

Micha looked toward the door, then squirmed hard enough that Colt just about dropped her. This little girl didn't seem pleased about sitting here and waiting, but as long as he could keep her quiet he'd be fine. So he reached for the cup of Cheerios, but as he did, Micha squirmed once more, slipped from his grasp and her feet hit the ground running.

He'd never seen a kid move so fast in his life, but instead of heading for the doors where her mother had gone, Micha dashed up the aisle toward the pulpit.

Colt's heart dropped. His gaze whipped between the door where Jane had vanished and then up toward that curly head of red hair that was bobbing past the pews and he slipped out of his seat. Ducking low, he dashed after her.

There was a ripple of laughter through the church as Micha got to the front, tipped her head back and gaped up at the pastor. She stood with her little legs akimbo and a handful of Cheerios clutched in one hand.

"…as the prodigal son…" The old minister stopped and looked down at his new arrival. "…as the prodigal… Hello, miss."

Colt arrived at that moment, and just before he could snatch her up, Micha zipped to the side and he was forced to jog after her, scooping her up a moment later. Micha let out a whoop of delight at this new, fun game, and Colt felt the heat of embarrassment blasting in his face. He stood there in front of the church, every single eye locked on him with this redheaded little girl perched in his arms. The fight seemed to have gone out of her, because instead of squirming and hollering like he expected, Micha took a single Cheerio between her fingers and pushed it between his lips.

"Num num," Micha said quietly. "Wanna Cheerio?"

Colt tried to keep his lips closed, but Micha was persistent, working that single Cheerio between his lips with a determination that was impossible to beat, and he finally took the Cheerio and grudgingly gave it a chew.

"Yummy," Micha whispered sweetly, seeming to approve.

"We've got a prodigal toddler there," the pastor quipped, and the church laughed. "And like a good father, Colt was there to catch her before it was too late.

God is a loving father, a good shepherd. He doesn't just give us up. Can I get an 'amen,' church?"

"Amen!" they called out.

"You're a good man, Colt," the minister said with a low laugh. "Faster than a greased piglet at that age, aren't they?"

"Sure are," Colt said, heading back down the aisle and wishing he could just sink into the floorboards instead. The other parishioners looked over at him, smiles on their faces. The older men chuckled in good humor, and Colt felt a wave of goodwill from his church family that he'd never experienced before. It was camaraderie, community, support. Was this what other people felt like when they had a family? The church all knew he was single, but it was funny how stepping into the expected role could generate so much support for a guy. Where was that outpouring of support for the singles? They didn't need it any less.

The door to the foyer opened and Jane appeared, her gaze landing on him with a look of surprise. She had Suzie on her hip, her hair flipped over the opposite shoulder. She was beautiful standing there, and his discomfort seeped away. He smiled sheepishly as he met her at the pew and they both slipped back into their spots.

"She took off on me," Colt whispered. "I wasn't quick enough."

"She does do that," Jane whispered back and she put Suzie down on the pew between them, then reached for Micha. "Were you being a stinker, Michal Ann?"

Micha looked at her mother innocently as Jane scooped the toddler into her lap, deftly clamping a hand down on Micha's chubby leg to hold her still. So that was how it was done.

"I think you were," Jane whispered, but there was a smile tickling the corners of her lips. "Be nice to him, Micha. He's not used to this."

Jane smiled and he felt that sense of camaraderie again. It felt good coming from her. It wasn't about pleasing a group or fitting in… It was just a moment between the two of them. Of all the people in this church who had known him for years, Jane probably understood him best.

And that was dangerous ground.

Chapter Nine

The next morning dawned overcast and cool. It was a relief after all of the heat they'd had lately, and Jane bustled in the kitchen, wrapping up lunch fixings to carry with them on their horseback ride today. Jane wore a pair of jeans and a pink T-shirt, and glancing outside she had to wonder if she'd need the sweater she'd set aside. It was hard to tell.

"Some crackers, maybe?" Peg said, pulling down a box from a cupboard. "Oh, here is some cheese you could cut up. And some apples—"

Peg was dressed a little nicer than usual—slacks and a crisp green top. Her hair was held back with two barrettes, and more time than usual seemed to have gone into the styling of it.

Jane accepted the box of crackers and poured a few into a bag. But as she worked, her mind kept going back to her time in church yesterday, Colt next to her, the girls between them… It had been too comfortable, she realized now. Colt was easy to be around. She liked him too much. If she had less of a friendly connection with him, it might be easier…if he were a little less good-looking, too. But a tall, ruggedly handsome guy sitting next to her as the girls played quietly, a guy she wanted to open up to who felt comfortable telling her about his tough stuff as well—it reminded her of the masculine support she'd been missing these last few years. It was that very support that she didn't want to get used to.

And she was about to go on a morning ride with the man... But she was looking forward to more than his company. She hadn't been on a horse in years, and she'd been missing riding a lot lately. It would be wonderful to be on horseback again.

"Should I just slice up a few apples for you?" Peg asked.

"Thanks, that would be great," Jane said with a distracted smile.

"You okay?" Peg asked.

"I'm just chronically tired." She shot the older woman a grin. "So what will you do while we're away?"

"I thought I'd help down in the canteen," Peg replied, then she turned quickly and walked toward the fridge.

"Oh, yeah?" Jane tried to smother a smile. "I heard the new cook is a nice guy."

"Very nice. I handpicked him. I'm sure he could use some help, though. And since you'll all be gone, I thought—" Peg put some apples on the counter, and her gaze flickered in Jane's direction irritably. "Why should it matter what I do?"

"It doesn't," Jane said quickly. "I'm sure he'll appreciate the help."

Peg didn't say anything else, but the knife hit the cutting board a little harder than it needed to with every chop, and Jane tried not to smile. Maybe Colt had been right about his aunt's interest in the new cook. And what should it matter? Just because Jane and Colt were avoiding marriage didn't mean that Peg had to.

The side door opened, and Colt appeared carrying two little riding helmets.

"Safety first," he said, kicking the door shut behind him.

The girls, seated at the table with scrambled eggs in front of them, perked up at the sight of Colt. They seemed to sense that they were going to have an interesting day, because the minute they saw the helmets, they forgot about their breakfast and wanted to go investigate.

"No, you need to eat," Jane said, catching Suzie as she slid down from her chair. "Come back. Breakfast first."

"Sorry," Colt said, and as Micha came around the table, he caught her with one muscular arm and dropped her back into her seat. "Listen to your mommy. She's the boss."

Micha stared at him for a moment, then made a move to get down again.

"Hey." Colt grew serious, and Micha froze. "Mommy's the boss. Look. I'm going to sit down, too. We've got to do what she says. There's no other way."

He sank into the seat opposite them, and Micha looked properly impressed and didn't make any other move to escape.

Jane shot Colt a grin. "Thank you."

"Just stating facts." But a smile tickled the corners of his lips.

The girls finally ate the last of their eggs—one of their favorite breakfasts—and they were ready to go. Jane grabbed the two plastic grocery bags filled with lunch fixings and the necessities she'd need for a few hours out with the girls—sippy cups of juice, diapers, wipes, a couple of blankets. A mom never knew how much of what she brought would be needed.

"See you later, Peg," Jane said.

Peg gave a curt nod, and they headed out to the truck.

"What's with Peg?" Colt asked, pulling the door shut behind them.

"She's going to see your new cook today," Jane said with a small smile.

"Oh…" Colt glanced back toward the house as he pulled open the truck door for her. "I don't get the problem."

"She likes him, and I asked about it," Jane said. "I think she's just a bit nervous."

"Huh. I think she's wearing makeup," Colt said, waiting as Jane buckled the girls into their car seats that were still in the back of the truck from their trip to church.

"And if you're wise, you'll never mention it," Jane said with a laugh.

Colt slammed her door shut and Jane adjusted her position while she waited for him to get settled in the driver's side.

"I'm looking forward to this," Jane said. "I haven't been on a horse since before the girls were born, and I miss riding."

"How often did you ride before that?" Colt asked. He started the truck and backed out. Jane could see Peg watching them leave out the side window.

"Whenever I could," Jane replied. "I had a friend from church who worked at a rescue ranch, and I used to come and ride with her, just to give the horses some attention and to keep them used to being ridden. I loved it."

Colt shot her a smile. "Good. This is an easy ride, but I think you'll like it, then."

They arrived at the barn, and Colt parked the truck then nodded toward the corral. "I just need to saddle them up. You ready?"

Colt led the way into the barn, and while he saddled the horses, Jane got the girls into their riding helmets. In years past, riding had been her escape, and part of her was hoping for that feeling of momentary freedom again. That rescue ranch she used to ride at had rescued more than horses—it had been the place where she found some calm and happiness with her husband stationed overseas. It had rescued her, too.

When it was time to get into the saddle, Colt brought a chestnut mare to the mounting block. Jane picked up the twins, just to be safe, and went around to the horse's head to say hello.

"She's beautiful," Jane said.

"She's gentle," Colt said. "I think you'll like her."

"I can mount on my own," she said. "But could you hold the girls until I'm up there?"

Colt stood back while she swung into the saddle, then handed the toddlers up to her one at a time. She held them both while he mounted his horse, and then he leaned over and took Suzie out of her arms.

"Let's see how this works," he said.

Jane settled Micha in front of her on the saddle, and Colt did the same with Suzie. The girls squirmed a little at first, but they soon got the feel of riding and Jane smiled over at Colt and Suzie, who looked like they were enjoying themselves, too.

If she was looking for freedom, she might not find it. Motherhood changed what freedom was possible, although those tethers were welcome. She looked over at Suzie held so gently in front of Colt, and she felt a wave of maternal satisfaction.

"I think we're ready," Jane said, patting Micha's little belly. Micha grabbed onto Jane's hand, small fingers clutching hers in excitement.

"I think we are, too," Colt replied, shooting her a grin. "Let's ride."

Colt set a gentle pace. They weren't in a rush today, and with the girls along for this ride, he didn't want to take any chances.

The day was cool, which made for a pleasant ride, and as he settled into the rhythm of the horse beneath him, he held Suzie comfortably in place. She looked around herself, babbling in half baby talk. He could only understand a few words of her chatter: horsey, bump-bump-bump, Mama... Whatever she was saying, she was having fun, and he felt his mood lighten in response to her babyish happiness.

The first few minutes of riding were noisy with toddler chatter, but as the ride wore on, both girls got quieter. The path he was taking was away from the pasture and through a rockier terrain. The grass was tougher and the trees were more plentiful—copses of trees spreading across the landscape. They were headed toward a patch of dark green—"the forest," as he and Josh had called it back then. It wasn't much of a forest, but there was a lot of denser growth out there and the trees grew tall and sturdy, unlike the bent, twisted trees they were passing here.

He turned, looking back at Jane, who was riding a couple of yards behind him, and he reined in slightly so that she could catch up.

"It's beautiful out here," Jane said.

"Yeah, I always did like this ride," he agreed. "Josh and I used to come out here when we were kids—back when you could let your ten-year-old ride and tell him to be back by supper."

Jane smiled sadly. "I can't imagine doing that with my girls."

He looked down at the toddler in front of him. "Well, they're pretty small right now. A different time, I guess. Besides, my mom knew I'd be fine with Josh. We were pretty resourceful together."

"You don't talk about your mom too often," she said.

"Not much to tell," he said.

Jane eyed him for a moment.

"She wanted this," he said at last. "Me to inherit. She thought after all the hard work I'd put in, I deserved it."

Colt felt a knot settle in his stomach. He hated the way it sounded—like they'd planned this somehow. It hadn't been that way, but his mom had mentioned it often enough that he had to wonder if she had suggested it to his uncle at some point.

"Your mom never did marry again after your dad left?" Jane asked.

"No, she stayed single," he replied.

"And she managed by herself…" Jane's voice was quiet and he glanced over at her. Was she looking for some sort of reassurance that it was possible to raise her children alone?

"It helped that Mom could work at the ranch," Colt said. "Although, it probably didn't help her relationship with her sister. They would have gotten along better with a little more space between them. They tended to judge each other a lot. Mom thought Sandra was too hard on Josh. Sandra thought Mom was too much of a free spirit. Sandra always did feel responsible for her..."

"The sisterly dynamic," Jane said with a small smile.

"Yeah, I guess so."

"What about your dad?" she asked. "He never contacted you?"

"A few times," Colt said, and his mind went back to those stunted phone calls when his mother would stomp out of the room to listen from the other side of his bedroom door. "Dad wasn't sending any money, so Mom was furious with him. She'd call him up every few years and demand some child support, and he'd have some excuse not to give it. But he'd talk to me on the phone then...ask how I was doing. Call me a good kid, even though he had no idea if I was a good kid or not."

"Would she have been happier if she'd married again?" Jane asked.

Colt shrugged. "I doubt it. Mom didn't think too much of marriage. She said it was just a contract, a piece of paper. When Dad left her with me, she was a wreck for a while. At least that's what Sandra told me. So Beau and Sandra gave her a job so she could get on her feet, and it turned out to be longer term than anyone intended."

"So that came from her," Jane said quietly.

"What came from her?"

"That idea that marriage is only a piece of paper."

He paused for a moment, the realization settling into him. Yeah, he'd first heard that idea from his mom. He could remember being a kid—ten maybe?—and his mother sitting on the steps to Beau and Sandra's house. She'd had a can of pop in one hand and deep sadness in her eyes. He couldn't remember what had just happened—his dad refused to send money? Or maybe Beau and Sandra fighting again? *It's just a piece of paper, Colt. Don't let anyone tell you otherwise.*

"Yeah, I guess so," he admitted. "But just because she recognized it first doesn't make it wrong, though. As much as we might want it to, marriage doesn't make people love each other. My dad was legally wed, and he took off." The wind picked up, and this time it had an earthy scent to it. "And look at Beau and Sandra. I mean, don't get me wrong, they actually stuck it out together, but they didn't like each other. At least not far as I could remember them."

To the east, Colt could see the outline of Josh's grandparents' old cabin peeking out from behind a spread of trees. It was deteriorating quickly these last few years, but there was a time when he used to like to ride out and look at it. They weren't his blood relatives, but he still felt a connection to them. His mom's father had been an alcoholic, and she'd never told a happy story about the man. Sometimes it was easier to connect to Josh's family. They seemed worthier, somehow. Even if that was unfair.

"I don't agree with her," Jane said, and he could hear the disapproval in her tone and he understood that. People didn't like to look ugliness in the face. And maybe most people didn't have to. He didn't seem to have a choice anymore.

"Look around you, Jane," he said. "I mean, not here." He laughed quietly. "But I mean at the relationships around you. I've got several friends who got divorced.

They just grew apart, they said. And I was a guest at those weddings. I saw how in love they were at the start. I even felt a little jealous watching them dance and stare adoringly into each other's eyes. It didn't last. Five years, seven years pass, and they change their minds. A piece of paper doesn't stop that from happening."

"Just because some marriages go wrong doesn't mean that God isn't offering something incredibly beautiful in the institution," she countered.

He couldn't argue with that. She was right, but how could anyone know if their marriage was going to soar to the great heights of what was possible in God's plan or nosedive with the others? He rode along in silence for a few more minutes. That cool wind was getting ever stronger, and he glanced up at the overcast sky. Were they in for rain today, after all? It was still hard to tell. Sometimes these threats of rain could sail right on overhead and hit another area.

Jane rode along next to him, her gaze turned away so he couldn't see what she was feeling. Micha was nodding off against her arm, and he glanced down to see that Suzie was getting pretty dozy, too. There was something about that rhythm on horseback that worked like a lullaby.

"I'm not saying happily married people don't exist," he went on. "I'm just saying that a piece of paper doesn't guarantee anything. It just locks people down, makes them financially obligated toward each other."

"I *wasn't* locked down," she said, turning toward him again.

"But were you *happy*?"

A fat drop of rain hit his hand, and he tipped his hat up, looking at the darkening clouds.

"It's starting to rain," Jane said.

"Sure is," he agreed, and he reined his horse in. "I want to hear you fess up—tell me the truth. Were you happy with my cousin?"

Jane reined in her horse, too, so that it pranced around in a circle to come close to him again.

"The girls will get cold," she said, and she turned to pull a small blanket out of her saddlebag. "I've got some little blankets for them, but—"

"There's an old house over there," he said, pointing toward the old cabin. "We can wait out the thunderstorm there."

Jane met his gaze for a moment and he could read the pain in her eyes. The wind whipped her hair around her face, and she handed the blanket to him and then reached back again for her saddlebag.

"I'll get it," he said, easing his horse forward and reaching into the bag for her. He pulled out another small blanket, and they both tucked the fuzzy blankets around the girls.

Then he nudged his horse around, and they headed into the wind and toward shelter.

"No, I wasn't," Jane said after a moment, raising her voice above the wind.

"What's that?" He looked over at her as another couple drops of rain hit the brim of his hat.

"I wasn't happy," Jane said. "Not…as one would describe it. But I was hopeful. I think that matters more."

And maybe it did. He wasn't trying to tear apart her memories or tarnish anything for her. What kind of guy would that make him? All he was wanting was for her to understand where he was coming from, because his position was a lonely one.

People wanted romance, marriages that lasted, and they kept on trying for it. And yet he couldn't quite forget that feeling he'd had in church on Sunday, sitting next to this beautiful woman as they kept the toddlers occupied. It was that feeling of togetherness, tenderness, that people chased. What guy didn't want the pleasure of a life with a woman as beautiful as the one next to him? What man wouldn't want to call her his?

But marriages always started out with that optimism, and he just didn't think it made sense to throw his own hat into that ring. After all, the unions he'd seen hadn't given him any hope that he'd fare any better.

Chapter Ten

The spatter of errant raindrops spurred Jane on faster toward the moldering house. Its roof was sagging in on one side and one of the windows was broken, but it would shelter them for the time being. Micha didn't seem to mind the rain at all and kept squirming a hand out from under the blanket, trying to catch a raindrop.

Jane had said too much. She'd never thought of herself as unhappy in her marriage to Josh before he died, because she'd loved him. It wasn't possible to love a man and be unhappy with him, was it? But after he'd died, she had been forced to admit to herself that she hadn't been happy. She'd been stressed, frustrated, wrung out…and that felt like a terrible thing to admit. She felt like she was letting Josh down, somehow. The things Josh had seen at war that changed him—those weren't his fault. But life together hadn't been easy, either.

Jane shouldn't have said anything. She should have kept that to herself. She looked up at the broiling clouds overhead—a downpour was imminent.

"There are some trees behind where we can tie the horses," Colt called, and she ducked her head and guided her horse around the side of the house. Colt was right—three very leafy trees grew close together just behind the house, and the horse didn't need any encouragement to move into the shelter of those low-hanging branches. Jane ducked her head to avoid being hit.

"Okay, Micha, you're going to have to hold on," Jane said. "I'm getting down first, and then I'll lift you down, okay?"

Jane swung her leg over and dismounted, but the minute she took her foot out of the stirrup, Micha held her arms out and launched herself toward Jane. Jane shot her arms out to catch her daughter with a laugh of surprise.

Colt rode up beside her, and Jane switched Micha to her hip and reached for her other daughter. Suzie was just blinking her eyes open again, looking groggy.

"Hey, you," Jane said with a smile, and as Suzie reached for her, Colt lifted her down into Jane's grasp. "You look tired, sweetie."

Colt dismounted and took the reins, then led both horses deeper into the shelter of the trees. Jane looked toward the house as a gust of rain-scented wind whisked her hair away from her face.

"It isn't locked," Colt said as he strode up beside her. "Let's get inside."

They burst through the door just as the rain started to hammer down. Jane looked around at a dusty, nearly empty cabin. There was a chair missing one leg leaning in a corner, and a small table sat in the center of what had once been a kitchen. Some dried leaves filled another corner beside the front door and the broken window, and at the far side of the room was an iron stove attached to a tin chimney.

She put the toddlers down, and they blinked uncertainly in the dim light and clung to her jeans.

"Who used to live here?" Jane asked.

"Beau's parents," Colt replied.

Jane took another spin around and spotted an old narrow staircase that led upstairs, but the cabin was tiny at best.

"How many kids did they have?" she asked.

"Six. But only the first four were born here," he replied. "Beau told me the stories about them. So did Josh, for that matter. This is Marshall pride right here."

Four children and two parents all in this one tiny cabin. It was hard to imagine being that cramped. But this was the site of her daughter's great-grandparents' home—so it was a part of their heritage.

"There's not a lot of space for that many people, is there?" she said.

"It was a different time, I suppose," he replied. "They had different standards."

Micha sidled away from Jane and headed for the closest window. She pointed outside.

"Horsey."

Suzie followed Micha and they both stood there in gray light by the dusty, rain spattered window, fingers pressed against the glass. Jane followed them and looked out at the horses. They were sheltered well enough under the trees and were eating oats out of feed bags. She turned back to the room and looked around.

"Can you imagine feeding an entire family on that stove?" she said, nodding toward the small iron stove on the other side of the room. "That would have been a lot of work."

She wandered over to the stove and tried to open the

oven, but the handle was rusted into place. With two girls of her own, she could only imagine how much work it would be to build the fire, cook the meals, keep the kids from burning themselves…

"It's not a lot of space," Colt said. "But considering they would have built it themselves, it's pretty impressive."

"It is." Jane's gaze stopped at a tarnished metal tea canister sitting on a shelf. She picked it up—it was empty. There was writing on the side she couldn't make out.

A family had lived here—a couple who had pulled together and started a ranch. It made her wonder about how their life had gone. One day, her daughters might ask about them, but they'd be more interested in the father they'd never met.

Guilt wormed up inside of her.

"I shouldn't have said what I did earlier," Jane observed quietly, putting the tea canister back on the shelf where she'd found it. "About my marriage. About Josh."

"Was it a lie?" Colt asked, fixing her with a direct stare.

"I don't lie," she said irritably. "It was just hard being married to him. That's all. And I don't think it was his fault. I think marriage is hard. I think it takes a reserve of character that no one realizes before they get into it."

"Very likely," he replied.

"Like this family that lived here all those years ago," she said. "They would have had a tough time. Especially in winter, and with baby after baby coming… It wouldn't have been easy for that mother, but life can be hard. And marriage can be hard, too."

"But back then, they had different expectations,"

Colt countered. "They didn't get married for the romantic reasons we tack on to the institution today."

"Says who?" she retorted.

"Come on! It wasn't about warm fuzzy feelings back then in a ranching community. There were a lot of practical things to take into account—including a woman needing a man to provide for her. A woman would have chosen her best option and gone with it."

"So you think this couple didn't love each other," she said.

"I'm not saying that. They probably learned to love each other," he replied. "But they wouldn't have expected all the warm fuzzies that we do these days."

"You can't know that," she countered. "There have been people who loved each other deeply all throughout history."

"Have they all been married?" he asked. "To each other?"

He was teasing now, but this wasn't just an argument for the sake of a debate for her. This mattered, because her faith was based on an understanding of things that included love in marriage. From Adam and Eve to Jacob and Rachel to Abraham and Sarah... Even Mary and Joseph! She'd struggled with Josh precisely because she wouldn't settle for less. She refused to sink into the background of his life and his heart.

But for all of her trying, it didn't seem to help much. And all of her trying had left her deeply exhausted.

"So what are you saying?" Jane asked with a faint shrug.

"I'm saying that marriage has been a lot of things, but romance hasn't always been part of it. Women were married off for family alliances. Men got married to

produce an heir. Sometimes you'd get a widow and widower who would marry just to share the workload to
feed their kids and survive winter!"

"I think God intended something more. Just because
humans have ruined something that God created doesn't
mean it's worthless," she said.

"What makes you so sure?" he asked.

"I can *feel* it," Jane said, putting a hand over her
chest. "Here. *I* can feel it. Women weren't created to
be sold off in blind marriages for political reasons. We
aren't just vessels for bearing children!"

"Hey, I'm not saying that," Colt said quickly. "I'm
just saying that marriage hasn't always been romantic.
I'm not saying that women should have been treated that
way. I'm against that, for the record. I think women deserve their freedom."

"Fine." She sighed and pulled her hair away from
her face. "It hasn't always been romantic." She didn't
know why this annoyed her so much, but it did. "But I
married Josh for love."

"I believe you." Colt heaved a sigh, then looked toward the window and the pounding rain again.

"And I'm willing to believe that the couple who lived
in this little house got married for love, too," she added.

"Yeah?" A smile curved up his lips again.

"Why…do you know otherwise?" she asked.

"Nah, no one told me how they met." He grinned at
her, and she felt her ire rise again.

"I'm not joking around, Colt."

"Jane, what does it matter?" he asked, the humor
evaporating. "You don't want marriage any more than
I do!"

He stood there, staring down at her with fire in

his eyes. He was standing closer to her than she'd intended, but the dimensions of this room didn't allow for much space. His arms were hanging at his sides, and he met her gaze, waiting for an answer with his eyebrows raised. She found her breath a little short, and she swallowed.

"No, I don't," she admitted.

"And that's okay," he said, taking a step back again. "Because if you look back on it, marriage was often just a piece of paper between a father and another man he was passing his daughter off to. And if you look at what marriage has become in our society, it doesn't last! But that doesn't mean that anyone was happier back when this cabin was a home. It just meant people didn't have an escape."

"Like your dad," she said.

Colt froze, and she realized she might have gone too far. His father's abandonment of his family shouldn't be part of her argument to make a point. She felt a well of regret at the words. She couldn't take them back, though, and they hung in the space between them.

"Would it have been better for my father to stick around and treat my mother the way Beau treated her sister?" he asked at last. "Because no woman deserves that!"

"There are other options," she said quietly. "I shouldn't have brought your father up, and I'm sorry about that. But there is the option to love someone. Stand by them. Be good to them, even when you don't feel romantic. That's an option, too."

"Yeah…" Colt sucked in a breath.

"Your dad shouldn't have left you and your mother," she said. "And Beau shouldn't have been so awful to

Sandra. They all should have been better to each other, kinder."

"You chose that route," Colt said. "You stayed with Josh and you loved him. But now that he's gone, you don't want to get married again because that was hard. And it hurt. And you'd rather be alone after all of that. So I'm not sure that your way was ideal, either. There was still collateral damage, wasn't there? That collateral damage was *you*."

Jane's heart clenched as his glittering gaze met hers. She looked toward the window again where Suzie stood with her palm against the glass.

Wait. Where was Micha?

She looked around the room, and there was no sign of her. There wasn't anywhere she could hide, was there?

Jane went to the staircase and looked up. "Micha?" She waited, listening. There was nothing but the sound of hammering rain on the roof, a distant drip from somewhere overhead. Nothing else. Jane looked back at Colt, dread rising inside her. "Did you see where she went?"

Colt strode to the staircase and went up, taking two stairs at a time. The wooden structure creaked under his weight, and he stopped at the top, ducking his head against the buckling roof. He could see the sky through a rather large hole, and the rain was letting up. The patter of raindrops on the wooden floor was gentler now. He looked around the second floor, scanning for signs of the toddler, but there wasn't really anywhere to hide. The second floor was nearly as empty as downstairs—an old iron bed frame leaning against one wall, a few paper bags from McDonald's crumpled up in a corner...

Those were from him and Josh visiting this place fifteen years ago!

His gaze snapped around the upstairs. There used to be a wall up here that separated some sleeping areas, but he and Josh had knocked it down one year for no reason at all. Just boys destroying stuff.

He wished he hadn't.

Colt came down to find Jane at the back door.

"Do you see her?" Colt asked.

"Nope." She scooped up Suzie and headed out into the rain. Colt jogged down the stairs and followed her outside.

"Micha!" he called. "Where are you, kiddo?"

"Micha!" Jane called.

The rain stopped nearly as quickly as it had started, and as he tramped through the long grass, he could hear Jane calling in the other direction.

Where was she? His heart hammered in his throat, and he sent up a silent prayer for help. The toddler was out here somewhere, because she sure wasn't in the house.

Colt circled around the front of the cabin, and he heard some rustling by the front step. Micha was crouching in the shelter of the overhanging porch, a caterpillar in her hands.

"Look!" Her face lit up when she saw him.

"There you are," he sighed, and beyond them, he could hear Jane's frantic call. "Mommy's calling you, Micha. Don't you hear her?"

"Mommy!" Micha called back cheerfully. "Mommy!"

Jane came around the corner just then, Suzie on her hip and her face white with relief.

"Micha! Where did you go?" Jane said, sinking down to her haunches and holding her free arm out.

"Look!" Micha said, marching toward her mother and holding out the caterpillar.

"Yeah, wonderful," Jane said, and her tone was so dry that Colt couldn't help but smile.

"That girl is a runner," Colt said.

"She is." Jane pulled Micha in a for a hug. "You stop running off, Micha. You worried Mommy."

"Oh, Mama…" Micha put a dirty hand on the side of Jane's face with a look of sympathy which immediately melted into an impish grin. "Look!"

She held up the caterpillar again, and Suzie reached for it, which brought on a squeal of upset from Micha, who didn't want to give up her prize to her sister, but the caterpillar was dropped. Jane sighed and stood up, leaving the girls to tussle at her feet.

"I feel a bit responsible for that," Colt said.

"Don't," she said with a sigh. "Apparently, I argue with you a little too easily."

The sun started to come out, and just behind her a rainbow came into view. Standing there with her hands on her hips, her jeans wet at the bottom from the rain-soaked grass and that dark gaze of hers locked on him, he found himself suddenly at a loss for words.

She was gorgeous.

She turned then and stopped.

"Look, girls, a rainbow," she said, then she glanced back at him. "You know how in the Bible it says that after the flood God sent a rainbow to reassure the people that he wouldn't put them through that again?"

"Yeah?"

"Sometimes I wish God would make that deal with

me," she said. "That I've experienced my worst. I won't have to go through anything that hard again."

Jane turned away again, not waiting for him to reply, and he watched her crouch down and point to the rainbow for the toddlers' benefit.

It was strange that they'd just argued about the value of marriage in that little cabin, and for what? She didn't want another husband, and he didn't want a wife. But there was something between them that didn't sit easily—maybe it was Josh's memory. Because he felt drawn to her for no reason he could see—just wanted to be with her, listen to her, help her out, and all they ended up doing was bickering because she wanted marriage to mean something, and for some reason that irritated him.

Maybe she was right and it had to do with his dad.

"Jane, I don't mean to keep arguing with you over dumb stuff," Colt said. "You should know that I don't go around picking fights with women on a regular basis. I'm normally a little more mannerly than this."

She rose to her feet and came back toward him. "I must be easy to argue with."

"You? No way. You keep winning," he said, giving her a grin. "Maybe I just care more with you."

"Why would you?" she asked with a shrug.

"Because I like you."

"Do you?" A smile came to her lips. "I used to be more fun than this, you know. I used to be more pulled together, too."

"I don't care. I like you this way," he replied.

"Even tired out, and my hair in a ponytail?" she asked with a teasing smile.

"Perfection." He took a step closer and caught her

hand in his. Her fingers were warm, and instead of pulling away, she squeezed his hand back.

"We aren't supposed to do this," she whispered.

"I know…" He wanted to move in closer still, but he didn't dare. "Maybe we can be friends who hold hands sometimes…"

"I don't think friends do that." She smiled slightly.

He dropped her hand, and his palm felt cold where her fingers had been. "Then I'll behave. But I stand by it, Jane. I like you. And I'm not hitting on you or asking anything from you when I say that. It's just a fact."

"That's the nicest thing someone has said to me in a really long time," she said softly. "But I'm so tired out. I'm drained. I feel like I've got nothing left to offer even a friendship anymore."

"You don't have to worry about that with me," he said. "Let me take care of stuff for a bit."

"For a few more days," she said, and she met his gaze. "Then we'll be signing papers and I'll be heading out. That was the deal, wasn't it?"

He paused. She was right. It was the deal, and he'd been trying not to think about it.

"Ever think about being a cook?" he asked. "You could stick around. Work the ranch."

"Your mom did that, and it wasn't good for the family," she countered.

"It would be nice to have you around," he said quietly. "Really nice."

"You hired a guy," she reminded him.

"I'm not attached to him yet," he said, and he sent her a teasing grin.

She sucked in a breath. "I don't know, Colt. I have a feeling that our bickering could get out of hand."

Colt nodded—he knew what she was trying to say. He'd like her to stay, and she didn't want to be in that close. It was okay. He didn't really blame her.

"So what do you want to do today?" Colt asked. "You want to keep riding, or go back?"

"I want to see that tree house, Colt."

"Yeah?"

"Yeah." She nodded. "This one's for Josh. I want to see what you guys were so proud of back then."

"Okay, then. Let's get back on the horses."

Micha and Suzie came tripping toward them, and Micha held up a long, wriggling worm between two fingers.

"Look!" she said.

Jane made a face, and then laughed. "Yes, Micha. It's amazing."

And maybe it was best that Jane not stay here on his ranch, settle in, raise her daughters here...because while he knew all the logical reasons to steer clear of matrimony, she was the one woman so far to seriously tempt him.

She'd be heartbreak in the end, he had no doubt, but sometimes a guy walked into pain willingly because a woman made it all seem worth it.

"Let's get going," he said, and he started around the house toward the horses. They were half an hour away, and he was hoping some time with memories of his cousin would get his feet back on the ground.

Chapter Eleven

The countryside sparkled with drips of rain that clung to nodding stems and left the air smelling of damp earth. The clouds rolled away and some patches of blue sky and sunlight broke through, warming the air and their skin as they basked in those first luxurious rays. Even the horses seemed to perk up, stepping a little higher and tossing their heads.

The rest of the ride was a quiet one. Colt kept looking over at her, because now that he'd had the idea of Jane just sticking around, he kept imagining what it might be like to have rides like this one more often.

Suzie settled in front of him, the ride seeming to lull her into a quiet mood. These girls could end up being skilled riders, given enough practice and access to a ranch. Not that he had all sorts of free time to give toddlers riding lessons. Why was he even thinking about this?

Maybe when they visited once every year or two, he could take them all out riding then. That was more reasonable, but the thought was mildly depressing. They wouldn't remember him. He'd just be a guy in a few stories their mother told them—their dad's cousin. And what was that? Not even a terribly close relation.

Colt could see the trees coming up in the distance, and as they drew nearer, his memories of the place came closer and closer to the surface. Back when they were kids, this patch of trees felt like it was so far away from all the adult supervision they were used to. They felt dangerous and grown-up. There was no one to tell them to how to do anything, no one to overhear their conversation. And there was that testosterone-fueled part of both Colt and Josh that had responded to the freedom.

"It's just ahead," Colt said.

The tree line was bathed in late morning sunlight, and Jane looked in the direction he was pointing.

"It's quite far from the house and the barns and all that, isn't it?" she said.

"Yeah, it is," he agreed. "It felt even farther when we were young, though."

Riding out with smuggled hammers and nails, some purloined boards strapped into saddle bags—the difficulty had made it more like an adventure. If they'd had access to some suitable trees close by everyone else, they would have lost interest and certainly wouldn't have kept adding on to the tree house in their early teens.

"Just past this patch of trees begins Bruce's land," he said. "And there are some streams that flow through here that he wants to own. It's just good on paper—maybe he's thinking of selling eventually and if his land has those streams on it, it'll be worth more."

"It's all about money, then?" she asked, casting him a sidelong look.

"Most things are," he said with a lift of his shoulders. "That's how the world works."

"Contracts and money," she said softly.

"Hey, nothing lasts forever," he said. "People die. Land gets sold."

"Memories do," she said, turning toward him, her gaze glittering with suppressed emotion.

"What do you want me to do?" he asked. "Keep this strip of land because my cousin and I bonded out here?"

"Maybe," she said.

"Money factors in, Jane," he said sadly. "I have to pay *you.*"

She stiffened, then nodded. "Right."

"I'm not blaming you for anything. You deserve to have a piece of this, okay? I'm just saying, I have to be practical."

Besides, what was he supposed to do, keep some shrine to old times with his cousin? Because Josh had been ignoring his efforts to make contact. Josh hadn't been clinging to old memories. Whatever their relationship had meant to Colt, it hadn't been the same for Josh.

"I know I was wrong in how I handled things with your husband," Colt said. "But he betrayed me, too. He walked away. He wouldn't accept an apology. If he'd been willing to speak to me, I would have sorted something out with him. If he'd lived—"

And going off and dying like that had felt like the last of the betrayals. When his cousin died, there ended any chance they had of reconnecting. It was over—and he'd died still hating Colt.

"I'm rather ticked with him, too," Jane said. "But you aren't supposed to be angry with someone who dies, are you?"

"I don't know." They came closer to the tree line and Colt reined in his horse. "Seems to me it's natural to be a bit angry. We're the ones who have to go on without him."

Jane reined in her horse, too, and they looked at each other in silence for a few beats.

"You're the only one I can talk to about this who really gets it," she said.

"You've got to lose someone you really loved in order to understand it," he said.

"He could be hard to love," she murmured. "He wouldn't let you in close."

"He was like that," he agreed quietly. "Pushed people off when he was hurt."

She smiled faintly. "Was he always so difficult?"

"You have no idea."

And yet, that stubborn idiot had been Colt's best friend growing up, and when he left the ranch and cut them off, he'd torn out a piece of Colt's heart, too. It hadn't been a regular argument between cousins—this one had been a permanent goodbye.

And all because of money, he realized bitterly. *All because of land.*

Josh had taken his inheritance for granted, and he'd never known how much Colt wanted this land for himself. Colt had ridden herd, delivered calves, stayed up late and gotten up before dawn without once being hounded into it by anyone because this had been his chance to do what he loved—work as a cowboy. So when his uncle was willing to change that will, what was Colt supposed to do? It hadn't been about Colt's worthiness so much as Josh's lazy attitude toward the ranch work. Given a few years, Colt had fully expected his uncle to change that will again.

And still, Colt had refused to go to Uncle Beau and smooth him over again for Josh. Because Josh didn't deserve it, and God forgive him, Colt still stood by that. Josh's only claim on this land had been through the DNA in his blood, and not through his own sweat.

Colt cleared his throat. "Let's get the girls some lunch, huh?"

They dismounted, and the next few minutes were spent letting the toddlers run around, getting their picnic lunch spread out on a blanket. The horses wouldn't wander far, and he let them graze on their own. The little girls were hungry and sat right down to eat their lunch without any wandering off.

As Colt swallowed the last bite of his roast beef sandwich, his gaze moved toward the trees again. It didn't look the same as it did seventeen years ago. The opening that had been there before had grown over.

"I'm going to find the tree house," Colt said, brushing off his hands and standing up, "and then I'll bring you over."

"Sure," she said with a smile. "I don't dare take my eyes off these two. You go."

The toddlers were looking tired, and when Jane patted the blanket, they both laid their heads down then popped back up again. She patted it again, and down went those little curly ginger heads once more. This might take a bit, he realized.

So Colt headed into the treed area and turned in a full circle. It had been so long since he'd been out here, and yet he felt like he could shut his eyes and pinpoint the spot.

He tramped west about twenty yards, and then he spotted a huge stump he recognized. It was more overgrown than he remembered, and several saplings now grew from the center, but it was the same. Then he looked up.

The tree house wasn't quite as high as he remembered, but it was there. The carefully constructed floor that was nearly flat—they'd been proud of that. A rope ladder that used to hang down was now just one piece of rope with a knot in the end. The elements had taken their toll on the structure, but it was still intact. They'd said they were building this tree house to survive a tornado, but it had made it through seventeen years of neglect, and that was almost as impressive.

He picked up the remnant of rope and gave it a tug. It seemed pretty solid. They'd left a few things up there, and he was curious to know how much remained. So he grabbed the rope and one of the lower branches, and started to climb.

As his boots hit the wooden floor, he gave a little stamp, testing the strength. It had held up well, and he turned in a circle, looking around himself. He was high enough that he could see through some patchy trees toward the grass where the horses grazed and Jane sat on the blanket, the toddlers both with heads on her lap. He paused, looking at how the sun made her dark hair shine in glossy waves. She was looking down at her children, and there was something in her posture that made his heart soften.

When he sold this piece of land, it would benefit her, and that made this worth it. She needed more support. Josh was gone… It wasn't like Colt had a family looking to him, nor would he ever. And he wondered if he could do a little more for her than simply buy her out for the cattle.

Not that she'd let him, he realized. Who was he fooling? Just because the sight of her made him feel things he shouldn't didn't mean she felt the same.

He turned his attention back to the tree house and rummaged around until he came up with a metal box he recognized. He pried it open and sorted through a collection of a few baseball cards, some polished rocks, an old report card that Josh hadn't wanted to show to his parents...

Colt smiled, his eyes misting.

"Back when our biggest problem was bad grades," he muttered to himself. That was one thing they had in common—neither of them had been great in school.

Underneath the report card was a set of dog tags, and he pulled them out. He couldn't remember where Josh had stumbled across these. A secondhand store, maybe? But he'd brought them up to the tree house, and they'd talked about becoming soldiers. For Colt it was just make believe. For Josh, it had been more.

At the very bottom of the box was another piece of paper, and Colt didn't recognize it until he'd unfolded it completely.

"The Good Cowboy."

It was a piece he'd had to memorize for church one year, and he'd been a nervous wreck. He hated speaking in front of people, and he'd brought that page up here to practice with his cousin.

It was a rewriting of the twenty-third psalm, describing God as the Good Cowboy instead of the Good Shepherd. It just made more sense to folks out here who raised cattle. God was like a cowboy who went after that lost calf, who shot wolves who tried to attack them, who led the cattle to the lushest valleys where they could graze undisturbed. God was the Good Cowboy who sang lonesome ballads at night, a gun over his knee and his watchful eye ever on the herd. He still remembered a few lines from it—that was how hard he'd memorized this old piece.

Colt straightened and looked through the trees again in time to see Jane looking around. He waved, and she spotted him then stood up, shading her eyes. The girls both seemed to be resting. They were both on their sides, their legs tangled together, but still.

She waved again, and he looked down at the box in his hands. She might want some of these trinkets. Maybe they'd mean something to her.

Jane saw Colt disappear from view, and she stood there on the blanket, waiting. After a couple of minutes she turned back to the girls again.

They'd both fallen asleep, but not too deeply. They might not sleep for long, but they'd be more cooperative with full stomachs and some rest.

A rustle in the trees drew her gaze, and she saw Colt coming out. He took his hat off and slapped it against his thigh as he approached, walking with the easy confidence of a man used to working outdoors. He held something under one arm that she couldn't quite make out.

"They're sleeping, are they?" he said when he came up.

"For a little bit. Trust me. This will make everything easier."

"I believe you." He smiled and those warm, dark eyes met hers for a beat.

"What's that?" She looked down at the box in his hands.

"Just a few of our treasures from back in the day." He opened it and passed her a piece of paper. "That's Josh's report card."

She scanned the grades—two Cs, a D and an F. "He hid it, then?" she asked with a small smile.

"Yep. He knew his dad would be mad."

Jane looked toward the trees again. This had been where her husband had grown up. She'd seen a handful of pictures from his childhood that his cousins had posted online—kids standing together, squinting into summer sunlight in front of giant bales of hay or at a birthday party wearing party hats and holding cupcakes… He'd always just been a kid in a group, but out here, it was different. This was the place that meant so much to him, that he wouldn't really talk about besides saying that treehouse was their masterpiece…

But she couldn't go see it yet—not until the girls were awake.

"You want to sit down?" he asked, and he nodded toward a fallen tree a couple of yards off. It was close enough to the sleeping toddlers that she could keep an eye on them, but their voices wouldn't disturb them.

"Sure." She followed him over, and they sat down, side by side in the cool of the shade. She could feel the warmth of his leg close to hers, and she was grateful for it as a cooling breeze picked up and made her shiver. She looked toward the girls, who seemed comfortable in the warm sunlight.

"Can I see it?" she asked, nodding toward the box.

Colt hesitated for a second, then he passed it to her. It would be his personal memories, too, she realized. She sifted through the contents, her fingers lingering on a polished stone.

"He mentioned that box," she said softly. "He was still half convinced these baseball cards might be worth something."

"They aren't, but you're welcome to keep them," Colt said.

Jane gathered them up in one hand and looked down at them. Her husband had had so many memories on this ranch, and yet he'd never wanted to bring her here…

"Are you really angry with him, still?" she asked quietly.

"Yep. I am." But his voice sounded tight, and when she looked over at him, she saw mist in his eyes.

"What happened?" she asked quietly. "All I know is that Beau changed his will, and Josh had enough. He'd never been the son that Beau wanted. Josh said that his dad had been more proud of you than he'd ever been of him—"

"That's not exactly what happened," Colt said, his voice low.

"Then what?" she pressed.

"He—" Colt turned toward her, his expression grim. "He asked me to go tell Beau I didn't want to be in the will. I couldn't do it."

"The money?" she said, her stomach sinking. Had it really come down to cash, as Josh had said? Coming out here, meeting Colt herself, she'd seen a different man than that but maybe she'd just been naive.

"The money?" Colt barked out a bitter laugh. "No! Josh didn't want *this*, Jane. He thought it was boring, and he wanted excitement. For years I worked this ranch in his place. He was always too busy—cadets, school football, girlfriends—" He stopped. "Sorry."

"It's okay."

"He was too busy with everything else," Colt went on. "And I did the chores. I did morning chores and evening chores. I worked by the hour and helped my mom make ends meet. I did it because I loved it, and also because I needed to contribute at home, make sure that us staying in the in-law suite downstairs wasn't a waste to my uncle and aunt. And my uncle really valued my contribution. I was up in the morning ten minutes before he was. Josh had to be threatened and cajoled to do even the basic stuff. He said it didn't matter. He'd be the boss, so he'd be supervisory, anyway."

Jane winced at that. Josh had mentioned a couple of those sentiments to her, too. He hadn't liked ranching—he'd been clear about that.

"Thing is, I had a single mom," Colt said. "I didn't have the same chances he did, and when my uncle told me he'd rather leave the ranch to me in his will because he knew that I'd actually run the place, I—" He heaved a sigh. "I was grateful."

"I could understand gratefulness," she said.

"Yeah. I mean, when else was I going to have a shot at owning a ranch? I could work one no problem, and I'd made my peace with that. At least I'd be doing the work I loved, but to have a chance to own it? It was something I hadn't even dared to dream about."

"Until then…"

"Until then." He nodded. "And once you let yourself imagine something, it's hard to back off again."

"And Josh wanted you to give it up," she concluded.

"I *should* have," Colt said, turning away again. "I should have told Beau that it wasn't worth tearing apart the family over. I mean look at me—do I look like I've made my peace with any of this? But I didn't. All I could hear was my cousin demanding that I give up this chance at more than I'd ever imagined—actually having a stake in this place after all those years of work. I felt like I deserved it."

"You probably did," she conceded.

"Ah, but Josh did, too. For other reasons. He was born to it. I couldn't compete with that."

"If Josh had lived…" she began quietly. "Would you have changed your mind about that? I mean, with a little more time to think it over?"

Colt looked at her, his eyes clouded. "You mean, would I have handed the land over to him to make him happy?" He shook his head. "A ranch is more than a business, Jane. It sinks into a man's heart. It puts down roots. I'm sorry. I know how this makes me look."

"It makes you look honest," she said. "You could have told me anything else. You didn't have to admit that."

"Honest…" He reached over and took her hand. "For what it's worth."

It was worth more than he realized. This kind of honesty was what she'd been looking for in her marriage and had never found. She'd just wanted her husband to open up to her, trust her with whatever was going on inside him.

"Colt," she said, turning toward him. "You're a good man, you know."

"You think?" He squeezed her fingers gently. "I'm not so sure."

"You were two stubborn men butting heads." She shrugged weakly. "You wouldn't be the first."

Colt met her gaze. "There are consequences, though. And I had no idea how far it would go."

"He would have gotten the cattle, and you would have worked with him," she said, shaking her head. "You're a good man."

The pain in his eyes tugged at her heart. He looked so alone, so filled with grief and self-reproach. She wanted to make him feel better, and holding his hand didn't seem like quite enough. He turned away from her, leaning his elbows on his knees, and without thinking she leaned forward to kiss his cheek.

His gaze flicked at her as she leaned in, and he turned toward her. She froze—this hadn't been her intention, exactly, but as his dark gaze enveloped her, he reached out and put a callused hand against her cheek.

"Colt, I—" She was going to explain, but the words evaporated on her tongue and he leaned in closer, his mouth a whisper away from hers.

"You what?" he breathed.

She didn't answer him, and his mouth came down onto hers in a kiss. Her eyes fluttered shut as his lips moved over hers slowly, tenderly. The day seemed to evaporate around them, leaving her alone, his fingers tracing her jaw and his breath tickling her cheek. She could have pulled back at any moment—he certainly wasn't holding her there—but she didn't want to. When he pulled away, she sucked in a breath, feeling heat rush to her face.

"I didn't mean to do that," she said quickly, her gaze moving over to her sleeping daughters out of instinct and mild embarrassment. Of all the things for her daughters to see her do…

"I did," he said, his voice low and soft. "So blame me."

He reached for her hand again and twined his fingers through hers. His palm was rough and strong, and she looked down at their fingers, mostly as a way to avoid looking him in the eye after that kiss.

"We shouldn't be doing that," she breathed. "Neither of us want a relationship—"

"I know," he said, and he tugged her against his strong shoulder. "Chalk it up to all the things I shouldn't have done. But this one I'm not sorry for."

"No?" She leaned her cheek against his shoulder. Because she was.

"It was honest," he murmured.

It had been, and as she watched her little girls sleeping on the blanket in the dappled sunlight, she wished this moment could stretch out forever. It was so simple, so honest. It filled her heart in the most dangerous of ways, because it made her hope for things she knew better than to hope for… She was no naive girl anymore. She'd been through this, and she had two little children who needed her.

The only problem was that no matter how sweet and tender this moment was, it had no future, and a moment was all they had.

Chapter Twelve

That evening when Jane tucked Micha and Suzie into bed, there was no fuss—the girls were exhausted from both the ride out to the tree house and by the playing they did once they got back. There was something about that clean country air that seemed to do all of them good.

The toddlers curled up under the sheet and fell asleep almost immediately. Jane lay on the bed next to them for a couple of minutes while their breathing slowed, looking at those sweet little faces.

Jane had been trying not to think about that kiss, shoving it out of her mind and replacing it with work and forced smiles. But the truth of the matter was, she'd started it. She hadn't meant to start a kiss quite like that one, but she had been intending to kiss his cheek. Still not exactly appropriate.

But the memory of his strong hand cradling her cheek, his lips covering hers... She still got goose bumps. He was so strong and at the same time so gentle. She couldn't even blame him, and she halfway wished she could. Because that would be easier—pass the blame along and stop herself from feeling quite so responsible.

"What was I even thinking?" she murmured to herself as she got off the bed and stood up.

After they'd gotten back to the ranch, they hadn't spoken of it. Colt went back to work, and she did some cleaning out of another couple of bookshelves with Peg. Then there was dinner, when Colt came back, and idle chitchat about that stretch of land, the value of it and whether or not Colt would regret the sale. Mostly that conversation had been between Colt and Peg, and Jane had simply tended to her daughters.

That sale wasn't her business. This ranch wasn't her business. Most of all, kissing Colt hadn't been her business! And nothing she could do right now could make up for that kiss out there by the trees.

Lord, I'm sorry, she prayed, closing the bedroom door softly behind her. *Am I that lonely?*

And maybe she was. It had been three years since Josh's death, and even during their marriage she'd been lonesome. She'd turned to God, then, and let Him be her rock. So what was she doing now?

Jane ambled down the hallway toward the kitchen. She'd get a cup of tea or something, she thought. But as she stopped at the doorway, she spotted Colt at the sink. He started the water, then put in a squirt of dish liquid.

She paused there, watching him as he reached for a pile of plates and lowered them into the sink.

"You gonna just stand there?" he said, and Jane startled.

"I didn't know you heard me," she admitted.

He glanced over his shoulder and smiled regretfully. "I've made it weird between us, haven't I?"

"It was me—" She sighed. There was going to be no escaping this. She grabbed a dish towel off the handle of the stove and met him at the sink. "Look, I was as big a part of that kiss as you were, Colt. I'm not blaming you. If anything, it was my fault."

"So let's not place blame, then," he said. "We're both adults. We're obviously attracted to each other."

She didn't say anything to that, because there was no denying it. They'd been drawn to each other the last few days, and the end result had been an unforgettable kiss.

"So what did you think of the tree house?" he asked, changing the subject.

They'd gone to look at it after the girls had woken up. Colt had carried Micha on his shoulders, and Jane had held Suzie on her hip. They'd looked up at it from the ground, walked around the base of the tree. It wouldn't have been safe to go up with the toddlers, so she made do on the ground. She could imagine a young Josh up there, hammering away or just looking wistfully out into the forest… He'd always gotten such a wistful, sad look on his face when he thought she wasn't looking. Maybe it had started young.

"It's pretty impressive," she admitted. "Even now."

"Yeah, I think so, too." He pulled a clean plate from the sink. He rinsed it under some water, then handed it over. "It was nice to remember the old days when everything was uncomplicated."

Jane accepted the plate, then sighed. "I want my girls to have that—those uncomplicated years where a summer seems to last forever and life is easy. I mean, you never think it is when you're that age, but looking back…"

"They'll have it," Colt said. "You'll make sure of it."

"Yeah."

"And if you need anything, you'll tell me," he added.

"No, I wouldn't do that," she said quickly. "I can figure it out. Besides, with the money from the cattle, I'll be able to provide."

"I meant, if you need moral support," he said. "It won't be easy raising them on your own. Might be nice to have someone you can vent to."

"You're a busy man," she said.

Colt stopped washing and turned toward her. "Look, if you don't want my friendship, it's okay. But I want you to know that if you ever feel overwhelmed, or just kind of lonely—"

"Loneliness seems to be my problem lately," she said, cutting him off. "And it's made me do some stupid things."

"I thought we weren't placing blame." Those dark eyes met hers.

"We aren't," she said softly. "But we need to be more careful."

"I agree with that," Colt said, turning back to the washing. He rinsed another plate and put it into the sink. "I said before I wasn't sorry about it, but with a few hours to kick myself, well, I do regret it."

That was a relief. She couldn't be the only one to feel bad, because that kiss had been too sweet, too honest. She'd wanted that kiss, and she couldn't trust herself to turn down another one.

"I think we need to take a little bit of space from each other," she said.

"Space." His tone was hollow, and she couldn't tell what he meant by repeating the word.

"It might make it easier to get things onto a more even footing," she said.

"Jane, I don't know what you're worried about, but I'm not the kind of guy who would push himself on you. I'm sorry I kissed you. I shouldn't have. But you don't have to worry about me taking advantage, or—"

"It's not you I'm worried about," she said quickly. "It's me. I liked it. More than I should have. And apparently, I'm more vulnerable right now than I thought. Trust me, Colt. I know you're a good man, and I'm not afraid of you or anything. I don't trust myself right now."

"Oh," he said quietly.

Just like she seemed to do with this man lately, she'd said too much. She felt the heat come to her cheeks again, and she inwardly grimaced. She didn't need to tell him that. She could keep some dignity, at least! She dried another couple of plates, stacking them on the counter next to her.

"Hey, it's me, too," he said after a moment of silence. "I'm just as attracted to you. You're gorgeous, and you don't seem to know just how beautiful you are. It makes you…even more beautiful. But it isn't just your looks, Jane. You're sweet, wise, understanding… You're a beautiful person, not just a beautiful woman, and apparently, that's my weakness. Go figure. I've never stumbled across anyone just like you before. So, yeah. I get it. I'm attracted, too."

She glanced up at him from the corner of her eye and caught him looking at her.

"I'm not sure that helps," she said feebly.

"Oh. Well, the point I was trying to make was that you shouldn't feel stupid or anything. I'm there, too.

You're not alone. And we both know what we can give—there's no confusion there."

"No, there isn't," she agreed, and a wave of sadness swept through her. Whatever she was feeling here had no future. She needed to quash it now, before she got hurt. Except it might be too late for that. Driving away from this ranch was going to be difficult.

"I mean, this much cowboy… I get that I'm hard to resist." He grinned.

Jane laughed and smacked his muscular arm. "I'll find a way, I'm sure."

They both chuckled and Jane reached for another plate. They worked in silence together for a few minutes, their movements synchronized.

"I'm sorry that you have to sell that land because of me," she said as Colt washed the last dish.

"Don't be," he said. "That land means something to me, but it's in the past. Josh wasn't coming home again. I know that. Some mistakes have permanent consequences."

Some mistakes, like allowing herself to get emotionally involved with her late husband's cousin. She didn't want to ruin this friendship that had been developing. She needed a person in this family she could trust, who she could feel comfortable around when she brought her girls back to meet family from time to time.

Jane needed some calm, some stability and no more emotional burdens.

They'd shared a very mutual kiss, but if they were careful, they could put it behind them.

The next morning, Colt didn't come back to the house for breakfast. He texted his aunt that he'd be eating in the canteen so that she wouldn't waste her energy cooking up something big for him. But he was avoiding Jane. He could pretend that it wasn't that big of a deal, but the truth was, he hadn't kissed a woman in a few years, and that kiss had meant something to him.

It shouldn't. He knew all the reasons why it would never work. She was Josh's wife… She was looking for stability for those girls, not the mess that was left behind with Beau's death. And no matter what he was feeling for her—emotions he didn't dare name—he was supposed to be the strong one. Jane had been through the wringer already with a difficult marriage, losing Josh, raising twins on her own. Colt hadn't been rattled around as much as she had. He'd been actively avoiding that wringer, but with her, all those walls and defenses he'd built up over the years seemed to crumble.

Midmorning, Colt got a call from the lawyer saying that the paperwork was ready that put the land into his name, and the cattle into Jane's. He'd also drawn up the sales agreement for Colt to buy back the cattle at a fair price. All they had to do was sign it, and he'd owe Jane some cash. This should be good news—getting some red tape out of the way so he could talk to the bank about a loan…or sell that strip of forest. His chest ached at the thought of their time together coming to an end, and he rubbed the heel of his hand over the spot.

This had been the plan all along, and Jane was only here to speed up the process. Colt was owner now, and he could finally take the reins.

Colt dialed Jane's number and waited until she picked up.

"Hello?" she said.

"It's Colt," he said. "I just heard from Mr. Davis."

"Me, too," she said. "It looks like the paperwork is ready for us."

"Looks like," he said gruffly. "Maybe we could head down there this afternoon together."

"Thanks. That would be great." There was a pause. "A Mr. Armson came by. He's chatting with Peg right now in the kitchen. He wanted to see you."

The sale. Right.

"I'll come on up," Colt said. "Tell him to wait for me, if he can."

"Okay. See you soon, Colt." And her voice softened just a little when she said his name.

A few minutes later, Colt parked his truck by the house, right next to the big white Ford F-250 that his neighbor drove. It was shiny and new, a direct contrast to Colt's beaten-up old pickup truck. Bruce's ranch was doing better than this one—better management, maybe? That thought stung.

Jane was outside under the shade of the big tree, the girls digging in the dirt with what looked like kitchen spoons. She smiled and raised one hand in a hello.

"Hi," he said.

"Hi." She hooked a thumb toward the house. "He's waiting on you."

"Yeah, I know," he replied. "You looking forward to getting that paperwork out of the way?"

"Sure. Yeah. Sure." Her smile fell. "I'm going to miss you, Colt."

He nodded curtly a couple of times. "Me, too. But this isn't going to be instantaneous. I have to sell that land, get the money from Bruce, and then I can pay you. So even if you head on out, you'll hear from me again, at the very least."

"That's true." She smiled, then spotted a toddler taking off. "Suzie!"

Colt grinned as she jogged after Suzie, who was worming under the fence. Colt felt better somehow, just for the short chat with her. But he didn't have time to really think that over. Duty called. He headed in the side door, letting the screen slam shut behind him. Bruce sat at the table, a mug of coffee in front of him, and Peg stood by the counter, arms crossed over her chest.

"Hey, Bruce," Colt said, and Bruce rose slightly as they both shook hands. "Good to see you."

"Good to see you, too," the older man said. "I was just chatting with Peg here. Been too long since we caught up."

Colt smiled and nodded, then looked over at his aunt.

"That's my cue to leave," Peg said. "We'll chat later."

After Peg left the kitchen, Colt pulled out the chair opposite his guest and took a seat.

"So you're here about the land?" Colt asked.

"I don't want to put on pressure during a difficult time, Colt," Bruce replied. "But I've got a bit of a time crunch here on buying that land, if you're willing to sell it."

"Yeah?" Colt frowned. "Why's that?"

"I'm putting my ranch up for sale," Bruce replied. "And if I include that strip, I can sell for about twenty percent more."

"As much as that?" Colt raised his eyebrows, then let out a low whistle. That meant if he kept that strip of land, he'd be doing the same for his own ranch's land value. "But why sell?"

"It's time," Bruce replied. "I've got two kids, and neither of them are real interested in ranching for themselves. So if I sell now, I can put some aside for my own retirement and then split the rest between them. It would help them out while I'm still here to see it."

"Easy as that?" Colt asked, narrowing his gaze. Beau had a single son who'd had no interest in ranching, and he'd made a much different choice.

"Nothing's easy," Bruce replied.

"How many generations of Armsons have been on that land?" Colt asked.

"My wife's father owned it before me. How many generations of Hardins have been on yours?" Bruce countered.

It was a good point. Land changed hands every generation—that was just the way of the world.

"Before I inherited this place, there were three generations of Marshalls on this ranch," Colt said. "There's family history here."

"But not your family," Bruce replied.

No, not Colt's family in a direct line. The one who should have taken over the ranch didn't want it. And the man who died had been too stubborn to see past the dirt under his feet to the son whose heart he'd broken.

"There's personal history here, too," Colt said curtly. "I've worked this land since I was a teenager. I know every acre."

"I know that, too," Bruce said, softening his tone. "You're asking how I can do it—sell this ranch and act like it means nothing to me."

"I was wondering," Colt replied.

"Truth is, it hurts like crazy. I love my ranch, and I wanted my kids to love it, too. And they do…don't get me wrong. They just don't love the work. My daughter's a lawyer now, and my son is a digital artist working for a book company. I told them I wanted them to do what they loved—figured one of them would come back to cattle. What can I say?"

"I was hoping to have you as a neighbor a while longer," Colt said.

"Yeah, that would have been nice," Bruce replied. "But my body is caving in on me. I've got diabetes now. You know that? And the doc says I should get my knee replaced. That just feels so…old."

Colt smiled sadly. "Might want to follow doctor's orders, though."

"Yeah, yeah…" Bruce smiled faintly. "Thing is, I'm not getting any younger. My kids keep pointing it out."

"Okay," Colt said. "But if I sell to you, I'm making the land next to mine more profitable, and mine less."

Bruce nodded. "There's that. I wanted to be clear about it. I don't want to be taking advantage. I'm offering to buy a strip of land that would be valuable to me. I don't want to pull the wool over your eyes in any way."

Everything was changing. Even Bruce Armson, the one who seemed just a mite more blessed than everyone else, was leaving this area.

"Who are you considering selling to?" Colt asked. "Some corporation?"

"Nope, a woman who owns two other ranches in the next county. And she's looking to expand. She's not a corporation yet."

"That's something."

"Look, can I give you some advice?" Bruce said after a beat of silence.

"Sure," Colt replied.

"Things change. If you can accept that, it's easier. I don't think Beau dealt with that fact very gracefully.

He wanted to hold on to the old ways and keep it consistent. But nothing will stay the same. You'll buy some fields, sell some. You might even sell the whole outfit and do something else. What do I know? But that's life. The older you get, the faster the world seems to change around you."

"Is that meant to encourage me to sell that strip of land to you?" Colt asked with a wry smile.

"Nope," Bruce said. "I'd like to buy it, if it suits you. If you want to hold on to it, I'm still going to sell, just for a bit less. That's all."

If all were even, Colt would rather keep that land. Not only was it valuable for the water rights, but it meant something to him on an emotional level, too. But everything wasn't even. Colt had to buy back his cattle, and any more debt on his part would seriously threaten his ability to keep this ranch afloat. He sucked in a deep breath.

"I'm willing to sell," Colt said. "But I'm going to need a higher price."

Bruce smiled faintly, then nodded. "How much are you asking?"

The men settled down to hammer out a price. And as they went back and forth, Colt realized that he was every inch the owner of this place, and Bruce was right. Everything changed—it couldn't be stopped—but Colt yearned for something that wouldn't change. He wished there was something he could latch on to that would stay the same, or at the very least *stay.*

Hadn't that been the problem with Beau and Sandra? They'd started out loving each other, and something changed, turning them into two battle-hardened veterans. His own father hadn't stuck around. Colt had grabbed on to this land, hoping it could be the rock-solid foundation he was looking for but even this ranch would change… Today, it would lose a strip of land and some value along with it.

They came to a price they could both agree on, and Bruce stuck out his hand.

"Is that a deal?" Bruce asked.

"It's a deal." Colt grasped his hand and they shook. "I'll have a word with my lawyer about the paperwork."

Bruce rose to his feet and sucked in a deep breath, then released it. "I'm glad to have that out of the way, I have to say."

"I'll be sad to see you go," Colt said. And meant that more deeply than the older man probably realized. Bruce Armson was a pillar around here, and nothing would be the same again. Not with Bruce gone. Not with Beau's death. Not even with the land under his feet.

"I'll keep you posted on the sale of my ranch," Bruce said. "I'm sure we'll get you some decent neighbors."

"Right." Colt forced a smile. He was doing what he had to in order to pay off Jane for the herd.

Then she'd be gone, too.

Chapter Thirteen

"So it's final—you're selling that strip," Jane said as she hopped up into the truck next to Colt. The day was already hot, and she could smell the musky scent of his aftershave in the cab of the truck.

"Yeah, I am." Colt started the vehicle as Jane did up her seat belt. Peg had offered to watch the toddlers while they made this trip into town, and Jane had gratefully accepted. This would be an important appointment and two little live wires would only get in the way.

"I've said it before, but I am sorry," she told him. "I know how much that land means to you."

"Maybe it will help me to let Josh go," Colt said. "Everything changes, right?"

Jane fell silent as Colt headed down the gravel drive that led to the main road. He looked grim, and she wondered how much this sale was going to hurt him. Beau had meant well in leaving something to his son's family after all, but it still came at a cost to Colt.

"You know why Bruce wants to buy it?" Colt said after a moment.

"I don't."

"He's selling and wants his ranch to be worth more," Colt said.

"That's crass. What about the value of your ranch?"

"Yeah, well, at least he was up front about it," Colt replied. "Neither of his kids is interested in taking over the ranch, so he's splitting it up now—selling and giving them what he can."

"Oh…" She looked over at Colt. "What Beau tried to do, I suppose."

"In his own way. And a little too late."

"So this will be it, then?" Jane said. "We'll sign papers, and…?"

She wasn't sure what she was asking. It felt like something was coming to an end for them, and they both knew it. Real life was pressing in and whatever they had been entertaining between them would have to be stopped.

"I'll have him draw up a sales agreement for Bruce and I, too," Colt said. "I'm going to talk to the bank about a bridge loan. When I can show them the paperwork for the sale, hopefully they'll lend me the money to pay you sooner if I need it. It was something Bruce mentioned on his way out. He says it doesn't take too long—a couple of weeks."

"Oh." She nodded. "It's not a big rush, Colt."

"Yeah, I know, but I want you to know that you'll get what's yours." He glanced toward her, sliding his hand over the top of the steering wheel.

"I'm not worried about that. I know you're honest," she said.

"Good." He smiled at her, then reached over and took her hand. She'd been waiting for this, much as she hated to admit it.

Jane looked out the window, watching the telephone poles whisk past. His hand was warm over hers, his fingers callused and rough but so gentle that she felt almost cradled. She should pull back, she knew it. Holding his hand felt natural, but what friends held hands while they drove? What friends reached for each other like this? They'd slipped past friendship, and now their time together was wrapping up.

Jane had wanted to be able to raise her daughters alone, have no more pressure to maintain a relationship, no more worries about a man's happiness or what he was feeling. She just wanted to focus on what mattered most, which was bringing up her little girls right.

So how come she felt a strange, aching sadness at the thought of leaving this ranch behind? She was tempted to chalk it up to the lingering grief of losing her husband, but she knew better. This had nothing at all to do with Josh and the past. This was about Colt in the here and now.

She'd miss him. He'd sunk into a tender part of her heart when she wasn't looking, and there seemed to be no undoing it. She'd messed this one up royally.

"Colt, have we ruined any chance of being friends?" she asked hesitantly.

"Why?" he asked.

She squeezed his hand. "This."

"Oh, this…" He smiled faintly. "Yeah, I'll have to cut this out, won't I?" But he didn't move his hand, and she didn't move hers. "We'll be friends. If you need anything, I'll be here. I'll check in on you. You'll see."

It sounded so comfortable, and yet she knew it couldn't be that way. They couldn't just torment themselves in limbo like this. Leaving the ranch and going back to their separate lives was the key here. He'd forget about her, and she'd go back to relying on herself, instead of feeling the comfortable warmth of this cowboy next to her.

"Jane?" His voice was warm and low.

"Hmm?"

"Anytime you want me to let go of your hand, just say the word."

Jane smiled but didn't answer. She wasn't ready to let go. In the long run, she'd be fine. Her daughters would be provided for. They'd have a business they could all share when the girls were of age. Her daughters would be loved, fed, sheltered…and they'd have Colt and Peg, too. It might not be the big rambling family she was hoping for, but it was better than she had. She'd have to be more careful with whatever was happening here with Colt, of course.

It would be too easy to slide into a relationship that neither of them wanted. Someone was bound to get hurt. *She* would get hurt.

Jane pulled her hand out of his, and he froze for a moment then pulled his hand back into his own lap.

Colt didn't say anything, either, but she'd communicated her point. It didn't matter what they felt in the moment. She needed to stand on her own two feet. Falling in love with Colt would be the worst mistake she could ever make.

They signed the sales agreement for the cattle at the lawyer's office. Bruce Armson met them there, and he and Colt took care of their private sale at the same time. Then Colt dropped in at the Creekside Credit Union, and Jane waited across the street at a coffee shop drinking an iced Americano. When he came out of the bank, she met him by the truck and they drove back to the ranch.

Legalities complete—or almost complete. Colt was waiting for a decision on that bridge loan so he could pay her for the cattle that were currently in her name. Then they'd be done.

Colt went back to work when they returned to the ranch, and Jane fed her daughters a snack and cuddled them to sleep for their nap. The girls were extra cuddly; Micha fell asleep with her arm wrapped tightly around Jane's neck, and Suzie had hold of Jane's hand so that she had to ever so carefully disentangle herself before she could get away and let the girls sleep.

Lord, please clear my mind, she prayed. *Help me to focus on what is most important in my life right now. Help me to keep my priorities straight.*

Josh had been difficult and complicated. If she'd met Colt first, she'd have married him in a heartbeat. She froze at that thought—was she really thinking that? But if she'd met him first, she'd still be naive and wouldn't have children yet, either. She'd be a different woman. Now she was older, wiser and a whole lot warier of marriage and relationships.

At least she knew better.

While the girls slept, she decided to carry out some old stacks of newspaper that Peg had hauled out of some storage space. They were bundled up with twine, but still heavy. Maybe if she expended her energy on some hard work, she could get her mind back on track.

Because the memory of the gentle pressure of Colt's hand around hers made her heart speed up, even now. And that was not helpful!

Jane hoisted the first pack of newspapers and put

them down with a grunt. They were heavier than Peg had thought when she bundled them up. Jane carried them across the kitchen before dropping them to the floor in order to open the side door, then she hoisted the package again, pushed the screen open with the newspapers as she came outside and down the two stairs.

"You need a hand with that?"

She looked up to see Colt striding across the yard toward her. His hat was pushed back, and he moved with the easy grace of a man accustomed to physical labor. He didn't wait for an answer. Instead he picked up the newspapers in one hand by the knot of twine and carried them over to the woodpile.

"Thanks," she said.

"Don't worry about carrying those out," he said. "I'll take care of it."

"I don't mind doing it," she said.

"Yeah, well, I mind," he said, but the hint of a smile on his lips softened his words. "You don't need to do that for me."

Jane met his gaze. "I'm pitching in."

"Okay…" He paused for a moment, his eyes moving over her face. "I got a call from the credit union."

"Oh?"

"They'll have the money in my account in ten business days," he said. "Then I'll pay you."

"Oh!" Jane nodded a couple of times. "As easy as that?"

"It would seem. We've already signed for the sale."

"Right." She felt a rush of emotion pass through her. This was it—the fresh start she and her girls needed so badly. And yet, it also meant that her time here at the

Marshall ranch was through. "I suppose I should be heading out then. It's all lined up."

"You don't have to go right away," he said. "Why not stay for a few more days? You could do some riding."

"This isn't a vacation, Colt," she said with a small smile.

"I want you to stay," he said, his voice dropping and those dark eyes of his locking onto hers.

"This was only for a short time. We agreed on that," she said.

"We agreed on that before we got to know each other better," he countered. "I want you to stay. As my guest, or as an employee—whatever keeps you here. I'm not ready to just stop—" He didn't finish the thought, and he broke eye contact then shuffled his boot in the dirt.

"Colt, this went further than it ever should," she said quietly. "It doesn't matter how we feel right now. We both know what we want for the long term. Don't we? I don't want an ex-boyfriend in my wake. I want a friend—the real kind."

"We've slid past that," he murmured, and he stepped close. "Way past it."

Her breath caught in her throat, and she looked up at Colt. His tender gaze met hers, and she didn't have it in her to look away.

"I knew better..." she breathed. "I never should have..."

"Hey, I knew better, too," he said. "But here we are. I told myself I just wanted to help you out. I wanted to make up for some of what you lost. I almost had myself convinced, too, but..." He brushed her hair away from her face and dipped his head down, catching her lips with his. Her eyes fluttered shut and Colt slipped his arms around her waist. She put her hands against his broad chest and pushed him back. He released her, his arms falling limp at his sides.

"You *have* helped me out," she whispered hoarsely. She wished she could lean back into those strong arms, but she couldn't. "You've been really nice."

"Is that what you think this is?" Colt asked bitterly, and Jane's heart skipped a beat in her chest. His glittering gaze drilled into hers, and he shook his head irritably. "Everything we've done together so far? This isn't a guy being neighborly, Jane. This is a man in love with you!"

As soon as the words were out, Colt regretted them. What good did it do to tell her how he felt? Except he hadn't been able to stop himself. He was nothing if not honest, even when it was better to keep his mouth shut.

"What?" she breathed.

Colt shut his eyes, trying to find that sense of self-control again, but it was gone. He'd said it because it was true. He shrugged helplessly. "I'm in love with you."

"Colt, don't say that." Tears welled in her eyes.

"Why not?" he demanded. "It's the truth!"

"Because it doesn't help us!" she retorted.

Maybe she didn't feel it. Maybe she could flirt and open herself up without too much emotional toll on her, but he wasn't made of the same stuff.

"Whatever this has been for you… I'm not the kind of guy who just plays around with hearts. I tried to keep my distance, but it just didn't work, and there's only one reason for that. So maybe it hasn't meant as much to you, or—"

"It isn't just you," she sighed, putting a hand in the center of his chest again. She didn't look up, and he put a finger under her chin to raise her face. Her brown eyes met his and he saw tears shining here.

"I didn't think so..."

"But loving you doesn't make this work!" she blurted out. "It only makes everything harder!"

"I need you around here. I don't want to just watch you go."

He stared down at this woman, her eyes glistening and his heart pounding with the force of his feelings. Why couldn't she understand that?

"And then what?" she whispered. "What happens then, Colt?"

"Then we don't have to say goodbye. We can...figure it out."

"Figure out *what*?" she demanded. "I don't want marriage, Colt! I've been the naive young thing falling in love and dreaming about happily-ever-after. But that isn't me anymore. Marriage is hard. It's draining. It's two people trying to figure each other out and never quite managing. I can't do it. I know what I can give, and I can't be a wife again!"

Her words hit him solidly in the heart and made his chest ache. "I know," he sighed. "But I feel the same way about what I can offer. I don't want marriage, either. I haven't been through the heartache that you have, but I'm equally scared of it. I don't think I could survive a divorce."

"So what happens if I stay?" she asked, shaking her head. "We try to be friends. We try not to hold hands when we drive somewhere together, and we pretend that we're nothing more than buddies. That wouldn't be better, you know."

He could imagine the torment of pretending not to love her—trying to fool himself and tamp down whatever feelings kept bubbling up inside him.

"Maybe not," he agreed. "I'm not sure I could stay away from you."

"We'd end up heartbroken anyway," she said, shaking her head. "This won't work, Colt."

"I know…" He put his hand on her cheek and she leaned into his touch. The last time he'd touched her cheek like this, he'd kissed her…and he was holding himself back from kissing her again.

"I'm going to miss you," he breathed.

"Me, too." She took a step back, and he dropped his hand. "Should I leave today? To make it easier?"

"No," he said gruffly. "I don't need it to be easier. Besides, it's already getting late. How far will you go? It'll be a hotel stay for nothing. Stay one more night and start fresh in the morning."

He wasn't ready to say his final goodbye yet, because once she had her balance again, would she even want him in her life? There were no guarantees. No matter how much he wanted to keep a connection between them…

Jane moved toward the house again, and she stopped at the door to look back at him. Tears shone in her eyes, and it took all of his self-restraint to keep himself from crossing the grass and pulling her back into his arms. But he stood there, stalk still and his chest aching.

She wasn't his to hold.

His heart just needed a little time to accept that.

Chapter Fourteen

Colt didn't mean to skip breakfast back at the house the next morning, but there was an emergency out in the west pasture. One of the ranch hands called him on his cell phone. But before he hit the gas to head out there, he texted Peg—I've got to see to a cow stuck in the fence. I'll be back as soon as I can. Tell Jane...

He stopped typing. Tell her what? Nothing that he could have his aunt relay. He erased the last two words and hit Send. Then he texted Jane directly—There's an emergency in the field. I'll be back in a couple of hours. If you're still here, it would be nice to say goodbye.

He hit Send on that text and waited for a moment. Would she answer? He hoped so. He'd been thinking of her all night, and he couldn't shake her out of his heart. He'd fallen for this woman, as hard as he'd tried not to. There was no immediate reply, so he dropped his phone in his pocket and put the truck into gear. Work on a ranch never slowed down for long, and right now that might be an answer to prayer. Because he'd prayed most fervently that God would take away these feelings for Jane. His decision to stay single had been a noble one, and he'd truly believed that God had been leading in that. There was a blessing for single people, too, because they could focus on things that family men couldn't. God needed the devoutly single as much as He needed the happily married. He'd felt that deep in his soul.

But pray as he might, on his knees in front of his bed, his hands clasped together as he begged God to just take it away from him, God didn't soothe his heart the way He normally did. That pain stayed, gnawing and deep.

So maybe this was His answer at long last in the form of work. Maybe it was best to get out there and lose himself in the job that he loved. Because he and Jane had said it all yesterday. There was nothing else to say that they hadn't already covered. Neither of them wanted marriage, and playing with emotions this strong was like playing with fire.

If they wanted to stay true to God and their moral convictions, they needed to take some space, no matter how much that might hurt right now.

The drive out to the west pasture took half an hour. Colt tried putting on some music, but all the country songs seemed like they were about Jane, and he flicked the radio off, preferring his own thoughts. He was the owner of this ranch now, and it would thrive or fail based on his sweat. He was thankful for this chance— deeply thankful—but it was hard to feel it right now past the ache in his heart.

When he arrived at the broken patch of fence, he saw the problem immediately. Two ranch hands were trying to calm a frightened steer—the fence wire pressing a deep trough in his neck. Colt grabbed his wire cutters from the glove compartment and jumped out of the truck.

This was the job—this was the life! He'd chosen this, even sacrificed his relationship with his cousin to get this. He should have trusted God to provide it for him, without getting between his uncle and cousin. But that was in the past now, and all he could do was try to do better in the future. He'd had no idea how bad the fall-out was going to be.

Something crinkled in his shirt pocket and he reached past his phone and pulled out that old creased piece of paper from the tree house box. He'd put it in his pocket this morning, and he slowly unfolded it.

The Good Cowboy.

The Lord is my cowboy, and He makes sure I'm fed and watered. I don't lack for anything—the hay and oats He sets out are just what I need. He puts me out to pasture when I need a rest. He stands there and watches me, making sure I'm healthy and strong.

He leads me down the paths where I'll have sure footing—not only for me, but because of who He is. When it's dark, when it storms, when I'm scared half to death, His strong hand comforts me.

At the end of the day, my feed trough is full and He rubs me down. My water bucket overflows. His goodness and kindness are with me all my life long, and I call this barn home because of Him.

Tears welled in Colt's eyes, and he stood there, the page in one hand and his jaw clenched against the rising emotion.

What wouldn't Colt do to protect one of his herd? What wouldn't Colt pay to buy them back again?

God loved him and cared for him more carefully than Colt cared for his cattle, and yet as he looked at that steer—now calm and grazing—he realized that from the steer's perspective everything had been scary and painful. Even Colt had seemed like a threat. And all of that had been to get the steer back into the right pasture where it would be safe and secure again.

Colt had been praying and praying for God to take away this heartbreak he was feeling, and God wasn't answering with comfort. Instead, Colt was flooded with memories of Jane—her eyes, her pink lips, the feeling of her hand in his…the smell of her shampoo, the way she smiled that special smile when she looked down at her little girls.

It wasn't only Jane who had been filling his mind and his heart all night and all morning. It was the toddlers, too. Micha with her fiery personality that matched those fiery curls, and Suzie who was quietly mischievous.

If he weren't so scared of falling into the same trap as his friends and family, he'd want nothing more than to marry Jane and be a dad to those girls.

When he thought of Jane as his wife, he didn't even think of her in a wedding dress. Instead, he saw her in blue jeans on horseback, that dark, mahogany hair of hers blowing in the wind as she rode. He could envision a life together so beautiful and full that it made his heart nearly burst.

But where was the guarantee? Wanting it this badly would only make a failed marriage hurt that much more. He wasn't sure he could recover after something like that. Besides, she didn't want marriage. He knew that.

The steer raised its head and looked over at Colt. The two stared at each other for a long moment, and then the bovine bent back down to grazing. Colt wouldn't steer his cattle wrong. If they trusted him, he'd guide them true and keep them safe.

"How much more would You, Lord?" he murmured aloud.

He'd been afraid of his family history and his complete lack of happily married role models destining him for the same heartbreaking failure, but if he was to be one of the grateful few with a loving, lasting marriage, then it would be because of God, not because of his own instincts. What if these feelings for Jane and the girls that he just couldn't turn off were God trying to throw a towel over his head and guide him past all the things that scared him most?

Colt wasn't supposed to be trusting the people around him to steer him right, he was supposed to be trusting God! If God wasn't taking away the love in his heart for Jane and the twins, then maybe God was chasing him into the right field. It might be time to stop fighting it.

And as that thought settled into his heart, he suddenly realized what he needed to do. It might not make any difference whatsoever for Jane, but it changed a whole lot for him!

I will fear no evil: for thou art with me.

God was a better cowboy than he was. Maybe, just maybe, Colt could get back to the house before Jane left...

Jane buckled Micha into the high chair next to her sister. The air-conditioned ice cream shop was a welcome respite from the heat outside. Peg had suggested the place—Creekside Creamery. She said that the ice cream here was best in America, made from fresh cream from local dairies, and Jane wouldn't want to miss it.

With her emotions raw, Jane didn't care if she ate ice cream or not, but she didn't want her own heartache to affect the girls and she figured they could use a treat. Besides, shouldn't they celebrate the inheritance just a little bit?

And if she had to be brutally honest with herself, perhaps there was a small part of her that wasn't quite ready to leave Creekside. Perhaps there was another part of her that needed to soothe her broken heart, and chocolate ice cream had always been her first stop in years past. She might as well start there now.

Jane had two baby cups of ice cream in vanilla, and a medium cup of her own. She handed Micha and Suzie each a spoon. They could feed themselves now—they'd be covered from eyebrows to shoulders with ice cream, but that was half of the experience, wasn't it?

Jane sat down opposite the girls and let out a long breath.

"Let's say grace," she said softly, folding her hands. "For this ice cream we are about to eat, make us truly grateful. Amen."

Then she put the bowls in front of each girl. "Yum."

They knew what ice cream was, and Jane guided their spoons a couple of times before they stuck their fingers into the cups and slurped them clean—the preferable way to eat ice cream, it seemed. Jane took a bite of her own, her heart weighing heavier in her chest.

It was better this way—leaving without another painful goodbye. She caught Micha's cup just before the toddler threw it, and she scooped up some ice cream and popped it into the little girl's mouth. Micha's eyes lit up.

"Mmmm," Jane said, and she took a bite of Micha's ice cream, too. The vanilla was very, very good.

The girls wouldn't remember this, but she would—all these times when they enjoyed something together. This was the groundwork for raising two well-adjusted, well-loved girls. She'd be here for them, and she wouldn't be distracted with a demanding marriage. Her girls would never have reason to complain that she wasn't there for them every step of the way.

Jane turned to Suzie and scooped some ice cream into her mouth too, and as she looked up she saw an older couple come into the shop. The man was on crutches and his face on one side was badly burned—so much so that Jane startled when she saw it. He wore an army hat, the kind veterans wore. She was about to look away when she noticed how the wife walked slowly beside him, pulling coins out of her change purse as they made their way to the counter. The man said something, and his wife looked up at him, her eyes sparkling.

Jane paused, watching them.

The wife—she was wearing a wedding ring—put her hand on his, and Jane saw that his hand was equally scarred as his face—three fingers missing. The older woman turned to the teenager working the register and gave an order, then she started counting out coins.

The order was two small cones, and when they had them she carried them to a booth in the back, and her husband hopped on his crutches next to her. When he sat down, the wife raised the first ice cream cone to his scarred lips and he took a bite.

"Good?" Jane heard her voice as it filtered over

to where she sat. Then she took a bite of her own. "Mmmm. This is great, isn't it?"

There was some quiet chitchat that Jane couldn't make out, but watching as the wife tenderly feed her husband his ice cream, she felt tears rise in her eyes. This woman's husband had made it back from the war, by the looks of things. Jane's husband had not. Jane had received her husband's remains and a folded flag. A thank-you for her husband's sacrifice.

But what if Josh had come home? What if he'd made it back and she'd had the chance to spend more time with him, take care of him, get over those strange distances between them and find some closeness again?

What if she'd been able to go out for ice cream with Josh and her girls?

She would have been grateful for the chance at a life as a family. Even if it would have been hard. Even if Josh would have had his own personal torments she couldn't fully understand.

The wife reached forward with a napkin and dabbed her husband's lips. He said something, and his eyes softened. The wife's low laugh could be heard from their booth, and Jane smiled in spite of herself.

This couple had been through misery, and they'd come out the other side. The woman laughed at her husband's jokes. The husband looked at his wife with eyes full of love. Had they always been that way, or had they grown into it after the hardest of times?

But Jane hadn't had that time with her husband—the chance to grow from their struggles instead of simply feeling consumed by them. She'd never had the chance to get to the sweet spot in her marriage, and looking at that couple with their ice cream, she felt the depth of all she'd lost.

Tears welled in Jane's eyes and she blinked them back.

She'd been so afraid of marriage again because all she'd known was the hard part—the work, the feeling of failure, the heartbreak. But what if there were a man she loved enough to get over the tough times when they presented themselves and travel with toward that sweet spot?

What if she could have a chance at marriage again with a man like Colt? She'd be willing, she realized in a surprised rush. She'd be more than willing—her whole heart would be in it.

But Colt had his own heartache, and he wanted marriage even less than she had. Colt couldn't be the man to grow old with, no matter how much she loved him. If there was one thing she'd learned from her marriage to Josh, it was that one person wasn't enough to carry a relationship. It was too heavy, too tiring. A woman's love couldn't rescue a marriage if the man's heart wasn't in it. She wouldn't try to be enough for two again.

No, it was better to go back to Minneapolis to start over again. It would take time to get over Colt, and very likely he'd be the guy she measured all the others against going forward. But the thought of marriage wasn't quite so scary anymore. If she could find a love like that older couple, she'd stand by her guy.

She was doing the right thing in leaving Creekside.

Lord, provide for us, she prayed. *And give me the strength to raise my girls right*.

When she'd given Micha and Suzie their last bites, Jane pulled out some wet wipes and cleaned their sticky fingers and faces. Her girls were the center of her world, the center of her heart. They deserved all the love and energy that she had inside her. They were her most sacred duty.

"Time to drive," Jane said, and she swallowed back the emotion that rose within her because she knew who she was leaving behind, and the image of that tall cowboy had slipped into her heart.

They'd start over, and God would provide for them. Maybe He'd even provide her another husband one of these years. Regardless, God was the One she could depend on.

Chapter Fifteen

Colt arrived at the house to see Jane's car was gone. He pulled off his hat and ran his hand through his hair. He was too late, and his heart felt heavy and sodden inside him. He could text her later. He could call her even. That was something. But seeing her one last time—that would have been better.

"Oh, there you are," Peg said, opening the side door. "High time, too! Jane and the girls left about half an hour ago."

"Yeah…" Colt nodded. "I'd hoped to talk to her."

"You might have hurried a little more then," she retorted, then rolled her eyes. "I mentioned Creekside Creamery, by the way. I suggested the girls might like some ice cream before she headed out of town."

"Oh yeah?" He perked up at that. There was a sliver of hope here…

"For what it's worth," Peg said, shooting him an annoyed look.

Peg didn't hide her feelings well, and he'd managed to disappoint her. It would have to wait. He hopped back into this truck and started the engine.

"I'm going to town," he called out his open window. "If anyone asks."

Peg smiled at that. "I'd speed a little, too, if I were you."

Colt did drive faster than usual as he navigated those familiar roads that led to town. He needed to lay eyes on Jane, see her face. It might not change anything—in fact it probably wouldn't—and maybe this was just an indulgence on his part but he had to talk to her.

He focused on the road, tapping irritably on the steering wheel as he drove. The miles clicked by on the odometer, and when he finally entered Creekside's town limits, he felt a little bit better.

Maybe she wouldn't even have stopped at Creekside Creamery. Maybe she just drove on through, putting Creekside, the Marshall ranch and Colt all behind her. But then again, maybe she hadn't...

Creekside Creamery was in the downtown, and as he stopped at each intersection, he wished he could just plow on through. But the ice cream shop finally came up, he turned into the little parking lot that was shared between it and the hardware store and he spotted her car.

The back door was open, and Jane was bent over, reaching inside.

"Thank You," he breathed, in a quiet prayer. She wasn't gone yet!

There was a spot next to hers, and he pulled in. He hopped out of his truck and slammed the door, then leaned against it as he waited for her to finish what appeared to be the buckling of car seats. She finally emerged, and her eyes looked red rimmed. She didn't look up at him until he said, "Jane..."

And then she raised those teary eyes and blinked at him in surprise.

"Colt? What are you…" She shook her head. "I was just thinking of you."

So those tears had been for him. He was going to say something—explain himself, maybe—but instead he found himself closing that distance between them and covering her lips with his. She leaned into his arms, and she felt perfect there, warm and soft. When he finally pulled back, she blinked up at him.

"I had to see you," he said. "Peg mentioned Creekside Creamery and I decided to give it a try. I'm glad I caught you."

"Why?" she asked, shaking her head.

"I miss you already?" He smiled faintly. "I just… Jane, something's changed. And I don't know if it will mean anything to you, but I had to tell you."

"What?" she whispered, those tear-filled eyes searching his.

"I was out in the field helping this steer that was stuck in a fence. That's why I couldn't come back for breakfast and to see you. Anyway, I was praying that God would empty me out of this love I felt for you, and… It was one of those God moments when I suddenly realized that maybe the love I've been trying to shake was God's intention all along. I am in love with you, and I've been so scared that marriage and family would be doomed to failure, but I've been looking to myself to be wise enough, strong enough, emotionally intelligent enough… and I'm not! I've never seen a functional marriage up close before. But if God has been guiding me to you, then I'll trust God to guide me the rest of the way, too."

"The rest of the way...where?" Jane asked, frowning slightly.

"I'm not trying to pressure you," he said quickly. "Oh, Jane. That's the last thing I want to do. I know you don't want another husband. I get it. I respect that! I guess, I just felt like you would be the only one to understand this, and...and maybe you'd see what I saw. Maybe you'd be willing to reconsider."

His words evaporated, and he looked at her helplessly. And he didn't want to say goodbye. Even now.

"I was praying for the same thing," Jane said softly. "And I've come to a realization of my own. There was this old couple in the ice cream shop—the kind that looks so happy, you know? The kind you wish you could be one day. I was married for such a short time, and when Josh died, we were still in the middle of a rocky patch that seemed to start right after the honeymoon. It was so hard. It was so painful, and I've never felt so lonely. But if he'd lived...if he'd come home injured instead of dying, I'd have taken care of him and felt blessed to do it!"

"I know," Colt said. She'd been a good wife to Josh. There was no doubt about that.

"But listen." She put a hand on his arm. "I've been so tired, and I figured that marriage was just too much work to interest me again. Except I forgot about the sweet spot. When a couple really love each other, when they get past the patches of hard work, they get to this place where they understand each other, and they've stopped accidentally hurting each other. And it's beautiful. Josh and I never got there. But I think I'd like to try to get there. I would."

Colt's heart hammered in his chest, and he caught her hand in his. "Wait… Jane, are you saying you'd be open to marriage again?"

Jane smiled, then shrugged faintly. "With a guy I loved so much he'd be worth the work, yes."

He slid his other hand behind her neck, tugging her closer. "Do you love me enough? Because I love you heart and soul. And if you'd be open to it, I'd propose right now."

"You would? But you said it was just a piece of paper." A smile curved up those beautiful lips.

"And that piece of paper wouldn't hold us together," he said earnestly. "God would. Jane, marry me. I mean it. I'm in love with you, and I really believe God brought us together. And I don't want to say goodbye ever again. I want to be all yours, and I want to be a dad to Micha and Suzie. I want to take care of the three of you, and I promise you, Jane, I'll do everything in my power to make sure it isn't work for you. I'll listen. I'll adjust. I'll take your advice. We can even build a little cottage for a bed and breakfast for you to run. You don't have to give up anything to be with me—I promise you that. I'll make it my life's work to make our relationship as sweet as possible for you every single day. If you'll just marry me."

"A bed and breakfast, too?" she asked, shaking her head.

"Why not? It would be our start—together. What do you say? Marry me?"

"Yes!" she said, and tears misted her eyes. He pulled her close again into a kiss, until they were interrupted by the babbling voices of the toddlers in the car.

"Mama? Mama? Mama?"

Colt broke off the kiss and rested his forehead against hers.

"Come home with me," he breathed. "You can stay in Beau's place upstairs, and I'll stay in my place downstairs until we can arrange a wedding. I'm pretty sure Peg would lend a hand there, too."

"That sounds really nice," Jane said, nodding quickly.

"Let's go home, then," he said.

He didn't want her to leave ever again. And he'd meant what he'd said about making sure their marriage was sweet and soft and tender. He wouldn't make things hard for her—how could he? He loved this woman with all his heart! He'd talk. He'd open up. He'd listen when she told him about her feelings.

Marriage didn't have to be hard on a woman, not when a man was making it his choice every single day to love her well. Jane deserved the best of him, and she'd get it. So would her little girls. He'd never put much stock in marriage before, but suddenly he couldn't wait to say those vows and get that piece of paper that reflected what his heart was doing this very moment— claiming them as his.

Epilogue

On a warm August Saturday, Jane and Colt stood in the minister's office of Creekside Country Church. Jane's heart was light in her chest, and she squeezed Colt's hand, her engagement ring still feeling new against her fingers.

Peg sat in a chair to the side, Micha and Suzie on her lap, and Paul stood behind her, a proud smile on his face. Peg and Paul had finally admitted to dating—well, "courting," they called it. And Peg had positively glowed when Jane suggested he be included in their tiny wedding.

Colt's mom had come for the wedding, too, and she sat next to Peg, holding a camera in her lap.

The twins were in brand-new church dresses—pink this time, with matching pink bows in their hair. Peg had spent a good fifteen minutes that morning trying to get the bows to stay. She had taken her duties with making his wedding happen very seriously, and there had been very little for Jane to even do. The toddlers each held crackers in their hands to keep them occupied, but her daughters' wide eyes were fixed on her.

Jane knew she looked different today in her wedding dress. It was a knee-length summer dress, covered in lace and nipped in at her waist. And her heart was so full that she felt young again. Except this marriage wasn't a risk—not really.

Colt stood opposite her, his dark gaze locked on her with such tenderness that it brought a mist of tears to her eyes. He loved her, and she loved him. And this time, Jane would be entering into the sacred bonds of marriage with her eyes wide open.

It may be hard at times, but they'd get through it. Colt was worth it.

Besides, he loved her girls, and he was already talking about horseback-riding lessons, new clothes and fixing up a bedroom for them with bunk beds when they were old enough—all decorated in white and pink.

The minister's voice brought Jane's attention back to the moment.

"Do you, Colt, take Jane to be your lawfully wedded wife, in sickness and in health, for better or for worse, as long as you both shall live?"

"I do." Colt's voice was strong, confident.

"And do you, Jane, take Colt to be your lawfully wedded husband, in sickness and in health, for better or for worse, as long as you both shall live?"

"I do." Her voice caught in her throat, and Colt gave her fingers a squeeze.

"Now it's time to exchange the rings…"

As Jane pushed the ring onto Colt's work-roughened finger, she couldn't get it past his knuckle and he took over, twisting it on. There was no hesitation there. Then he slipped her ring on to her finger and their eyes met in that moment, the import of the moment settling over them. These vows before God would bind them together over the coming years, showing God and their community that they had chosen each other.

"I now pronounce you husband and wife." The minister grinned. "Kiss your bride, Colt."

And Colt did just that. He leaned down and caught Jane's lips with his as Peg laughed in celebration.

"We'll now just sign the marriage license," the minister said, and Jane looked down at the sparkle of gold on her finger.

"Let's make this legal," Colt said, taking the pen and signing his name where the minister pointed. "Mrs. Hardin. I like that."

Jane took the pen next, and she added her own signature, then she turned to Peg, who released the girls and they ran toward her. Jane caught Micha in her arms and Colt scooped up Suzie. They were a family—and even the twins seemed to like this new fact. Jane wasn't alone anymore, and her heart brimmed with gratefulness.

"Yum?" Suzie said, pressing a cracker against Colt's lips, and without missing a beat, he took a bite.

"Yum," he said past the cracker, and he sent Jane a grin. "I love you, babe."

Her heart was finally secure with this tall cowboy, and she had a feeling that sweet spot in their marriage was already starting.

"Smile!" Colt's mom lifted her camera and snapped a picture. "Lean in together now, and smile!"

Their wedding pictures would be off center and amateur, but the love in their eyes was unmistakable. Their wedding cake was homemade—a sheet cake with white icing and their names written in blue—and Micha would end up planting her hand right in the center of it.

Jane's wedding ring was a simple band of gold, but it would stay on her finger for the next fifty years.

And that piece of paper that bound them together as husband and wife would be tucked away in the wedding album. Every few years, Colt would pull it out and smooth his hand over the creases.

"Don't lose that," Jane would remonstrate. "It's a legal document."

But there would be a tender look in Colt's eye when he put it away again. Because it turned out that it wasn't just a piece of paper, after all. It was a piece of his heart, legally recognized by the state and the country and anyone else who cared to question it. And it was a piece of Jane's heart, too.

Marriage, Jane would discover, wasn't so hard, after all.

* * * * *

*If you liked this story, pick up the first book
in the Montana Twins miniseries
by Patricia Johns:*

Her Cowboy's Twin Blessings

Dear Reader,

Is marriage only a piece of paper? A lot of people argue that, especially if they've been hurt. But I believe that marriage is a whole lot more than just a legal arrangement. There's something about those vows... Before you get married, you love each other deeply and you'd lay down your life for that other person. But after the vows, it's like a circle closes. It isn't only about emotion, but something deeper. Some people believe that marriage is a sacrament, and I understand that! Marriage is challenging. It's beautiful. It's holy. It deepens and develops us.

In this book, I wanted to look at marriage—not just the wedding day—and what it means to me. I hope you enjoy this story, and if you'd like to connect with me, you can find me online at PatriciaJohnsRomance.com. I'm also on Facebook and Twitter.

Patricia

HIS SUITABLE AMISH WIFE
Women of Lancaster County • by Rebecca Kertz

Helping widower Reuben Miller care for his baby was just supposed to be a favor for a friend. But when Ellie Stoltzfus falls for father and son, can she win Reuben's heart, despite his vow that he'll marry again only to give his child a mother—*not* for love?

HER OKLAHOMA RANCHER
Mercy Ranch • by Brenda Minton

Paralyzed veteran Eve Vincent is happy with the life she's built for herself at Mercy Ranch—until her ex-fiancé shows up with a baby. Their best friends died and named Eve and Ethan Forester as guardians. But can they put their differences aside and build a future together?

HIGH COUNTRY HOMECOMING
Rocky Mountain Ranch • by Roxanne Rustand

When he starts his life over after a medical discharge from the marines, the last thing Devlin Langford wants is for his childhood nemesis to rent a cabin on his ranch. But pretty Chloe Kenner and her sunny smile might be just what he needs to begin healing.

WINNING THE RANCHER'S HEART
Three Brothers Ranch • by Arlene James

Barrel racer Jeri Bogman arrives at Ryder Smith's ranch claiming she wants to buy property, but she has another plan entirely. A tragedy in her past is shrouded in secrets, and growing close to Ryder is the key to finding the truth.

THE TEXAN'S SECRET DAUGHTER
Cowboys of Diamondback Ranch • by Jolene Navarro

When Elijah De La Rosa runs into his ex-wife—the one person he hasn't apologized to for his youthful mistakes—he's shocked to discover they have a five-year-old daughter. But can he convince her he's a changed man worthy of the title *daddy*...and, possibly, *husband*?

THEIR BABY BLESSING
by Heidi McCahan

After leaving the navy, Gage Westbrook adopts a new mission—fulfilling his promise to look out for the baby boy his late friend never met. But when he loses his heart to the child and his stand-in mom, Skye Tomlinson, will Gage gain an instant family?

———————

Get 4 **FREE REWARDS!**

We'll send you 2 FREE Books
<u>plus</u> 2 FREE Mystery Gifts.

Love Inspired® books feature contemporary inspirational romances with Christian characters facing the challenges of life and love.

FREE
Value Over
$20

YES! Please send me 2 FREE Love Inspired® Romance novels and my 2 FREE mystery gifts (gifts are worth about $10 retail). After receiving them, if I don't wish to receive any more books, I can return the shipping statement marked "cancel." If I don't cancel, I will receive 6 brand-new novels every month and be billed just $5.24 for the regular-print edition or $5.74 each for the larger-print edition in the U.S., or $5.74 each for the regular-print edition or $6.24 each for the larger-print edition in Canada. That's a savings of at least 13% off the cover price. It's quite a bargain! Shipping and handling is just 50¢ per book in the U.S. and 75¢ per book in Canada.* I understand that accepting the 2 free books and gifts places me under no obligation to buy anything. I can always return a shipment and cancel at any time. The free books and gifts are mine to keep no matter what I decide.

Choose one: ☐ **Love Inspired® Romance**
 Regular-Print
 (105/305 IDN GMY4)

☐ **Love Inspired® Romance**
 Larger-Print
 (122/322 IDN GMY4)

Name (please print)

Address   Apt. #

City   State/Province   Zip/Postal Code

> Mail to the **Reader Service:**
> **IN U.S.A.:** P.O. Box 1341, Buffalo, NY 14240-8531
> **IN CANADA:** P.O. Box 603, Fort Erie, Ontario L2A 5X3

Want to try 2 free books from another series? Call 1-800-873-8635 or visit www.ReaderService.com.

---

*Terms and prices subject to change without notice. Prices do not include sales taxes, which will be charged (if applicable) based on your state or country of residence. Canadian residents will be charged applicable taxes. Offer not valid in Quebec. This offer is limited to one order per household. Books received may not be as shown. Not valid for current subscribers to Love Inspired Romance books. All orders subject to approval. Credit or debit balances in a customer's account(s) may be offset by any other outstanding balance owed by or to the customer. Please allow 4 to 6 weeks for delivery. Offer available while quantities last.

Your Privacy—The Reader Service is committed to protecting your privacy. Our Privacy Policy is available online at www.ReaderService.com or upon request from the Reader Service. We make a portion of our mailing list available to reputable third parties that offer products we believe may interest you. If you prefer that we not exchange your name with third parties, or if you wish to clarify or modify your communication preferences, please visit us at www.ReaderService.com/consumerschoice or write to us at Reader Service Preference Service, P.O. Box 9062, Buffalo, NY 14240-9062. Include your complete name and address.

LII9R

SPECIAL EXCERPT FROM

HQN™

Laura Beth is determined to leave Cedar Grove to find love and start a family, but then an Englischer and his baby are stranded on her property. Could her greatest wish be right in front of her?

Read on for a sneak preview of
The Wish *by Patricia Davids*
available May 2019 from HQN Books!

"What is that?" Laura Beth Yoder wondered out loud.

She stepped out onto the porch and folded her arms tightly across her chest. She closed her eyes and turned her head slightly, waiting for a break in the sound of the storm. There it was again.

It was a car horn. She was sure of it. Was someone in trouble? Lifting a raincoat from the hook by the door, Laura Beth pulled it on and zipped it up to her chin. She walked out onto the end of the porch.

Was she really going out into this storm? Whenever the wind died a little, she heard the horn again. It sounded like it was coming from the bridge.

The sight that met her eyes when she reached the top of the lane sent her heart hammering in terror.

A car had plowed into the rocky embankment of the creek at the edge of the bridge. The floodwaters swirling under it would continue to rise. They were already at the bottom of the car doors.

A dark-haired man sat slumped over the steering wheel. Blood trickled from his temple.

"Mister, you need to get out!"

He slowly raised a hand to the side of his head and blinked. She pulled on the door handle. It was locked. "You have to get out."

A high-pitched wail came from inside. She shone her light in the back seat. A baby sat strapped into a car seat. Water was already seeping inside the vehicle. She yanked on the rear door handle, but it was locked, too. The car shifted again. How long before the floodwaters swept them away? Was she going to watch this innocent child die?

She pulled on the door with all her might. It wouldn't budge.

She'd never felt more alone and powerless. Fighting down her panic, she searched for a way to break the glass. She hurried to shore, found a large rock and returned to the car. Praying the glass wouldn't injure the child, she closed her eyes and slammed the stone against the window.

Don't miss
The Wish *by Patricia Davids,*
available May 2019 wherever
HQN Books and ebooks are sold.

www.Harlequin.com

SPECIAL EXCERPT FROM

Love Inspired®
SUSPENSE

*When a guide-dog trainer becomes a target of a
dangerous crime ring, a K-9 cop and his loyal
partner will work together to keep her safe.*

Read on for a sneak preview of
Blind Trust *by Laura Scott,*
the next exciting installment in the
*True Blue K-9 Unit miniseries, available
June 2019 from Love Inspired Suspense.*

Eva Kendall slowed her pace as she approached the training facility where she worked training guide dogs.

Using her key, she entered the training center, thinking about the male chocolate Lab named Cocoa that she would work with this morning. Cocoa was a ten-week-old puppy born to Stella, a gift from the Czech Republic to the NYC K-9 Command Unit located in Queens. Most of Stella's pups were being trained as police dogs, but not Cocoa. In less than a month after basic puppy training, Cocoa would be able to go home with Eva to be fostered during his initial first-year training to become a full-fledged guide dog. Once that year passed, guide dogs like Cocoa would return to the center to train with their new owners.

A few steps into the building, Eva frowned at the loud thumps interspersed between a cacophony of barking. The raucous noise from the various canines contained a level of panic and fear rather than excitement.

Concerned, she moved quickly through the dimly lit training center to the back hallway, where the kennels were located. Normally she was the first one in every morning, but maybe one of the other trainers had gotten an early start.

Rounding the corner, she paused in the doorway when she saw a tall, heavyset stranger scooping Cocoa out of his kennel. Panic squeezed her chest. "Hey! What are you doing?"

The ferocious barking increased in volume, echoing off the walls and ceiling. The stranger must have heard her. He turned to look at her, then roughly tucked Cocoa under his arm like a football.

"No! Stop!" Panicked, Eva charged toward the man, desperately wishing she had a weapon of some sort.

"Get out of my way," he said in a guttural voice.

"No. Put that puppy down right now!" Eva stopped and stood her ground.

"Last chance," he taunted, coming closer.

Don't miss
Blind Trust *by Laura Scott,*
available June 2019 wherever
Love Inspired® Suspense books and ebooks are sold.

www.LoveInspired.com